While sketching the Temple of Dendur, graduate student Carter Denwright meets—and is seduced by—a powerful vampire by the name of Alder. Though immortals were once kept secret from the human world, now everyone knows of their existence. Blinded by mistaken feelings for Alder, Carter allows himself to be drawn into his life. Too late, he realizes two things: one, Alder is vicious and cruel, and two, Carter's true love is Alder's brother, Freyr.

The attraction between Carter and Freyr is strong, but they must fight this feeling or face the wrath of Alder. Despite their best efforts, Alder discovers the truth, and punishes Carter, hiding him from Freyr in a cruel game of cat and mouse.

Freyr is not as strong as his brother, but he vows that he will find Carter again and will stop at nothing to get him back. Carter, caught in Alder's cruel grip, commits an act of desperation that will change all their lives forever. The question is: can Freyr find Carter, and is the bond between him and Carter enough to break Alder's hold and spoil his plans to ruin them both?

Remember Him
Copyright © 2015 Kazy Reed
ISBN: 978-1-4874-3022-1
Cover art by Latrisha Waters

Published by eXtasy Books Inc or
Devine Destinies, an imprint of eXtasy Books Inc
Look for us online at:
www.eXtasybooks.com or www.devinedestinies.com

Remember Him
Amsel Clan Series: Book 1

By

Kazy Reed

DEDICATION

To MA Church and LM Somerton. It's their fault.

To Lisa, the best beta reader I could have had.

And to Jane, who was with me from the very first sentence.
You left us far too soon.

PROLOGUE

Secundus stood beside and a little behind his older brother, trembling in fear. He watched as Alder stood with his hands clasped behind his back, head lifted in defiance, his eyes glowing red with anger. A draft blew across the room and cooled the wet shirt that clung to Secundus' back. He shivered and focused his gaze on the spreading puddle of water at his feet.

This was not the first time the two brothers had stood in the great hall waiting to be punished for disobedience. Secundus knew they should never have gone into the town and caused such mayhem, but he'd often experienced the painful consequences of defying Alder, so he'd gone along with the plan, accepting the risk.

Their eldest brother, Lyulf, stood before them, hands on his hips. "Do you realize what you have done? What could have possessed you to put our clan in such danger?"

"We were hungry," Alder spat back. "I'm sick of starving in here when there is a banquet not ten miles away."

"Hungry?" Lyulf shook with rage. "Could you not control your appetite until you found a more inconspicuous place to hunt? The king will not let this pass."

"I thought you *were* the king," Alder scoffed.

Lyulf slammed his fist down on the table. "I have a mind to give them your heads!"

Secundus reeled back and stared in disbelief. Never before

had his brother spoken with such fury.

Lyulf's wife, Ershabet, stood and put her hand on her mate's shoulder to calm him. "You must control your anger. We have seen enough violence tonight."

"You are right, of course, my beauty." He took her slender fingers in his and kissed them. Taking a deep breath, he murmured, "Perhaps banishment would be better."

Secundus whimpered and fell to his knees. "No, no. I beg you, do not send me away. I need to be with my family. I will not survive alone. I committed the worst of sins, but . . ."

Alder laughed, then his smile turned to a sneer. "You talk of sin in *this* house? Always *so* righteous. Will you never accept that you have no soul?"

"I do not believe that," Secundus replied. "I believe we might still have a chance of redemption if we find a way to exist peacefully with humans."

Alder inhaled sharply. "Brother, a hunter must feed on its prey. Humans are rats, vermin unable to find enough dark corners in which to hide. We are the hawks, circling above their heads. Today we struck. Our talons sank into their flesh and their blood flowed. My lungs filled with the delicious scent of fear. My head swam with the shrieks of horror, the sweet song of children wailing for their parents. Such euphoria!"

Lyulf was disgusted. "Children? You murdered innocent *children?*" He roared and charged Alder, but stumbled to a stop when the door to the hall flew open and one of the stablehands ran in.

The boy collapsed into a chair. His shirt was awash in blood, his face ashen. He panted for breath. "*Mein Herr,* the southern wall has been breached . . . Guards have abandoned their posts. Gaelred has sent a hundred men from the North. We cannot defend ourselves against the knights. They number too many, even for us."

Lyulf looked to Alder. "What of our brothers? No news from them?"

"No," Alder replied. "Themus and Pieter went to feed yesterday, and they have not returned. I think that Helmut and Julius are still in Bavaria. There has been no word. Is that not so, Secundus?"

Secundus made no answer. The sounds of the mob grew louder as they neared the inner doors. Prayers and shouts of damnation echoed around them. Ershabet took Secundus in her arms. "Go with Alder. Take the tunnels from the south dungeons that lead into Kesseler Wood. They will not follow you there. We have never made your presence known. They will not hunt those that do not exist."

"I'm scared," Secundus told her.

Alder pushed him sideways. "This sniveling brat will only slow my progress."

Lyulf brought his hand across Alder's cheek and sent him staggering. Then Lyulf took him by the throat and growled in his face. "Our clan matters above all else, Alder. Take Secundus and rebuild the clan when you find others of our kind in the South. But you must swear not to leave our brother in danger."

"I swear it." Alder glared at Secundus with disgust.

The sounds of battering rams and axes intensified, and Lyulf ordered his brothers into the hidden chamber behind a large tapestry at one end of the Hall.

Ershabet turned to the stablehand. "Gather the servants and get out through the tunnels in the cellars."

He seemed dazed, and simply stared at his mistress. Lyulf cuffed him on the shoulder. "Do as you're told!"

After the boy ran toward the kitchen, Lyulf took his wife's hand. "Ershabet, my love. You must go with my brothers. Save yourself."

She recoiled, and her eyes burned with fiery rage. "I will

3

not leave my mate. If death is your fate, it is also mine. I will not spend a single day without you at my side."

Alder opened the hidden entrance to the tunnels. "Follow me, Secundus!" One last glimpse of his beloved brother and sister-in-law, and the heavy stone-and-wood door was pushed back into place. Secundus quickly began to pull up floor planks that concealed the ladder to the dungeons, but Alder grabbed his arm and snapped, "Be silent. I want to see what happens."

"You heard Lyulf's order. We must go."

"You go, then. I'm staying. There's a loose brick here some-where. Ah. Here it is."

He began to pull a long, thin stone from the wall, but Secundus protested. "No, Alder—"

Alder's blow knocked Secundus into the hard, rough-cut stone on the back wall of the small chamber. He felt his arm snap. Alder's satisfied grin chilled Secundus' blood. Although he was undead, the younger vampire knew that being under Alder's rule forever would be worse than death. He set the bone that protruded from his forearm. The skin over the wound burned like fire for a few moments while it healed, but it was nothing to what Lyulf and Ershabet were sure to suffer.

Secundus stood next to Alder and peered through the hole and into the great hall. The door of the hall crashed open. A huge swarm of men, all armed with bows and spears, filled the room. Ershabet showed her fangs and growled, but Lyulf put a hand on her arm to hold her back. Five priests wearing red pointed hoods and black robes entered behind the knights. One of the priests spoke loudly. "Lyulf von Drubich, son of the devil, we cast you back to Hell, and bring the Wrath of God down upon this house, with bow and spear."

"You shall not bring my house to an end," Lyulf said with a snarl. "There are more that will avenge me."

The priest stepped forward and removed his hood. With a

cold, deadly grin, he said, "Bring them."

Four men came in, each holding aloft a head of the absent vampires—Themus, Pieter, Helmut, and Julius. Secundus opened his mouth to scream, but Alder clamped his hand over his brother's jaw, forcing him to swallow a wail of anguish.

Ershabet wrenched out of Lyulf's grasp and ran at the priest. Before she took two strides, an arrow struck her in the chest. Another, and yet another arrow, brought her to her knees.

Lyulf roared more fiercely than a tiger. Even Alder quaked at the echoes of the call. Several humans fled, but priests showed no fear. With a nod from the unmasked priest, a soldier stepped forward and hurled a spear toward Ershabet. It pierced her gut, and she slumped over in a pool of blood. Lyulf gazed upon his slain mate for a moment, then seemed to come to some decision. Arms stretched out to the side, he stepped into the room, toward his beloved wife. The whip of flying missiles clawed at Secundus' ears as dozens of arrows struck his brother. Even after Lyulf sank to his knees, too weakened to threaten them, the humans riddled his body. When the assault finally ended, there were so many arrows in Lyulf that the wooden shafts held his body upright.

The priest took a long sword from his robes and held it aloft. "This house of Satan has been cleansed by the hand of God. I send you to burn in the pits of Hell forever." He swung the sword through the air, and Secundus watched as his brother was dispatched. Before Lyulf's head had stopped rolling, the priest brought the blade down again upon the neck of Ershabet.

Secundus felt as though the blade had pierced his own heart. The mob cheered and rushed toward the bodies, but neither he nor Alder saw the aftermath. They replaced the small stone and fled through the dungeons.

Germany, 1896

Heavy rains had blanketed the valley for five days. The normally tranquil stream that snaked around the ruined walls of Drubich Castle now rushed like a river, eroding the hillside and inundating the small town below. The grazing pastures at the base of the mountains were washed away, like dust from glass.

When the deluge stopped, villagers searched the forest, looking for any livestock that might have survived the flood. One farmer came upon a young ram that had fallen into a muddy pit. As he pulled the animal out, he lost his footing and fell forward onto something hard, half-buried in the muck. Digging through the soggy soil, he found himself lying atop a very large metal casket. The ancient, rusted hinges disintegrated with little pressure. He lifted the lid and gasped.

Six bodies had been shoved into the box. Their heads had been removed, and a wooden stake was driven through each heart. Crammed into what little space was left were the skulls, still covered with wiry locks of brittle hair. Around the inside of the casket were painted crucifixes and prayers in Latin, damning the devils buried within.

"Dear God in heaven," the farmer exclaimed in horror. *"Nosferatu!"*

Secundus flung the newspaper away as though it had burned him. His companion picked it up and chuckled. "Scary news this morning, eh?"

Secundus shook his head slowly and answered, "Stefan, I do not know what to make of it."

Stefan unfolded the paper and glanced at the headline. He collapsed into a chair. "Oh gods preserve us!" he breathed.

"What does this mean, Secundus? I thought the priests burned the corpses?"

"I didn't know what they did, neither did I wish to," Secundus snapped. "I was too busy running for my life."

The butler opened the parlor door, carrying a tray with tea and scones. He glanced nervously at his employer. "Would you like tea, sir?"

"Do we ever?" Stefan groaned. "Why do you do that, Lowner? Secundus and I don't eat. You don't have to, either. You're a vampire, for Christ's sake."

Lowner glared at him. "Please excuse my shortcomings, Stefan, but I'm a chef. I take pleasure in cooking. I enjoy sharing my creations with the others, and I daresay everyone else loves my cooking. However, since your diet is so limited, I'll refrain from offering you tea in future. You can fend for yourself in a back alley or brothel."

Stefan growled and waved him away. "Go polish something."

"Stefan!" Secundus snapped. He turned to the crestfallen vampire. "Forgive him, Lowner. We've just had a bit of a shock."

"Is everything all right, sir?"

"No. Everything is most definitely *not* all right. Look at the paper."

Lowner quickly scanned the article and put a hand to his chest. After a few moments, he laid the paper on the table. "My God, the exhibition is set to open in two days' time. Sir, have you considered your brother's reaction to this news?"

Secundus flinched. Of course he'd thought of how his brother would react. It would not be pretty. For over four hundred years, Secundus and his clan had lived in peace. The story of the Drubich vampires had, over time, corrupted into folklore. Everyone had heard the stories, but they were just fiction . . . or so they thought. The discovery of their brothers' bodies was Alder's chance to announce to the world that the myth was true — vampires did exist.

Secundus quickly pulled on his coat and called for his horse. Within half an hour, he stood on the steps of a horridly ostentatious mansion, waiting for his knock to be answered. After time passed with no response, he opened the door himself. A rank odor assaulted his senses. He held the back of his gloved hand to his nose.

Several men and women lay around the house, either in drug-induced stupors or post-coital fevers, their necks and wrists covered with drying blood. Some looked as fresh as plucked apples, still blushing with the excitement of bedding a vampire. Others looked haggard and seasoned — addicts, sated only temporarily by the pierce of fangs in their skin.

Any human brought to Alder's lair was quickly overwhelmed. His brother was legendary for his power of seduction. He fucked them, bled them, then fucked them again, keeping a cycle of pleasure radiating around the new recruits. Sexual deprivation and semi-starvation, rewarded with lavish banquets and orgies, kept his human followers hanging on his every breath, but they were not strong enough to realize Alder was torturing them. He was a master of his art.

Secundus paused at the sound of a low moan from the room to his right. He pushed open the door, but did not enter. A female vampire sat between the legs of a young man. He was all of maybe twenty years old. He writhed in the throes of passion while the vampire fed from his femoral artery. The man's body tensed as his would-be killer stroked his sex and sucked his blood. Feeling his fangs drop as his cock hardened, Secundus turned his eyes from the temptation and continued on his mission.

He called out, "Alder?"

"My dear brother!" Alder replied from an upstairs bedroom. "Come up here."

Climbing the stairs, Secundus grimaced at the sight of a liveried footman on his hands and knees on the floor in the hall. He was at the mercy of one of Alder's guards, a large Hessian named Max. There were stories of the unfathomable girth of Max's cock, and by the sounds of the footman's pained grunts, Secundus had to believe the stories were true.

Alder was much too careless when it came to hiding the vampires' existence from humans. Many humans already knew he was a vampire. In fact, several members of the local government were frequent visitors at this castle of sin. This day was no exception. A sickly sweet smell wafted from beneath the bedroom door. Secundus pushed it open slowly and gasped at the scene before him.

One of the local earls was stretched out on the divan, lazily sucking Alder's cock. Another earl moaned in ecstasy while the vampire drank his blood. A third man, whom Secundus did not recognize, lay in the corner, inhaling opium through an elaborate hookah.

Alder sat up and licked his lips. "Well, well. The prodigal son. Have you come to celebrate?"

The question did not bode well. "What is there to celebrate?"

His sadistic brother held the earl's head with firm hands and thrust into his throat. The young man gagged and choked as the vampire released his seed into the man's mouth. Alder finally showed mercy and let him go. Secundus scowled at the display.

"Please, brother, I beg you not to do this."

"Do what?" Alder replied with an impish smile.

"Announce our existence to the world. I know that is your plan. It will only cause us trouble."

"No!" Alder boomed. "For four hundred years, I have watched from the shadows while mankind flourished. Here is the opportunity to break free of our prison. Imagine the power we shall wield over them! Our brothers' bodies will be displayed as curiosities, sideshow relics, but even with such proof, men will not believe in us. I intend to change that. Soon they will all know vampires are not ridiculous somnambulists with long claws and bat-like ears. They will finally see our true forms. No, Secundus, I will have my day of glory. *We* shall have *ours*."

Secundus shook his head. "I want no part in your scheme. I wash my hands of it. No good will come of this, Alder. We coexist peacefully now."

"Always the peacemaker. Fine. Run back into your corner and sulk while I take back what is rightfully ours."

Two days later, the exhibit opened at the Berlin Museum. Hundreds stood in line for a chance to glimpse the bodies of the "Devils of Drubich," as they had been dubbed. Wealthy patrons of the museum and the city's most important families were allowed first access to the exhibition. As they filled the hall, the curator approached the dais to speak.

But he hadn't uttered a word before screams and shouts of panic rose from the street outside. The heavy doors burst open, and the audience fled to the corners of the room. Alder, followed by several members of his clan, strolled in and peered at the remains on display in the center of the space. He then spoke loudly, hands held high.

"I am Alder von Drubich." The spectators murmured in astonishment. The vampire smiled. "You have desecrated the grave of my beloved brothers and sister, exhibiting their bodies as freakish curiosities. The church once thought our clan had been destroyed, but they were wrong. The priests in Drubich did not know of my existence, or that of my brother, Secundus, who lives in this very city . . . but they will now."

The crowd gasped in shock. One woman wilted into her astonished husband's arms. The curator, when he found his voice, said to a few police officers present, "Remove this man. He's obviously deranged."

"I am no man!" Alder boomed. His fangs dropped, and he smiled. "There are hundreds of vampires on this continent. We are ready to be accepted into society. Ready to be honored, respected, obeyed. No longer will we live concealed, despised, vilified in ridiculous, fictional tales."

Removing his coat, as if he was a showman, Alder rolled up his sleeve and spoke again. "Here is your proof that I am what I claim." One of his entourage handed him a large hunting knife. Alder drew it deep into his forearm, hissing at the sting. Women screeched in horror, and men choked in disgust, as blood dripped down onto the floor. As they looked on, however, the horrible gash began to heal. The bleeding stopped, and the skin knitted over the wound, until no trace was left. Alder licked off the blood, bowed theatrically, and leaped all the way across the room. Humans fled in all directions, while he and his clan walked calmly out the door.

The news spread quickly throughout the city. Within hours, thrill-seekers began to gather outside Secundus' house, hoping for a glimpse of the vampires. Stefan looked out at the street from an upstairs window and scoffed. "Why can't I just go kill Alder? Maybe if I offer his heart to the museum to add to the exhibit . . ."

Secundus rolled his eyes. "I would say that was a good idea. However, my brother is the most powerful vampire in existence. Even you could not overcome him."

Stefan groaned. "What are we to do, then? We cannot stay here."

"I agree. We must leave," Secundus decided. He put his hand on the doorknob and turned back. "God knows what evil my brother has just unleashed."

One week later, in the dark of night, Secundus von Drubich

disappeared, never to be seen again.

CHAPTER ONE—CARTER

2011

The intense August heat had given way to a powerful thunderstorm. Rain began to pelt the streets of Manhattan, and I cursed. I'd planned to spend a nice, leisurely Thursday afternoon in the Metropolitan Museum of Art. Now tourists flocked into the building, seeking shelter from the weather. The relatively empty galleries began to fill with loud voices, and wet shoes squeaked on the polished floors.

"Great." I turned back to the Temple of Dendur and continued sketching the structure. I'd graduated from NYU in May, with a degree in Classical architecture, and the Egyptian Temple at the Met had always fascinated me. Built in 15 BC by a Roman governor of Egypt, it was decorated not only with beautifully carved hieroglyphs, but also with graffiti from the various visitors over the years.

Thunder echoed and lightning cracked through the black clouds visible through the bank of windows next to the temple. A group of school children raced around, chased by their harried teacher, desperately trying to quiet her charges. I rolled my eyes and resumed my drawing.

A few moments later, I realized the room had become very quiet. The thunder continued outside, but the voices of children no longer assaulted my senses. There weren't even any hushed exclamations of awe at the magnificence of the displays. I turned around and was shocked to find the gallery was completely deserted. A wisp of cold air raced up my neck, and I shivered at the sensation. What could have driven everyone away?

"That's a very good drawing."

The voice startled me. I spun around to find a man sitting next to me on the bench. I yelped in surprise, but didn't move from my seat. As much as his sudden appearance confused me, I found myself inexplicably drawn to the man. He was gorgeous — dark blond hair, blue eyes, chiseled jaw, with an amazing toned, lean body. This was the epitome of *my type* of man.

He raised an eyebrow and smirked. "Hello, Carter."

I blinked. "How did you know —"

"Name badge." He pointed at the ID hanging around my neck.

"Right." Feeling like a dork, I lifted the lanyard over my head and tossed it into my messenger bag sitting open on the floor. Glancing at my new companion, I bit my lip. "Who are you?"

"Alder Eberly," he replied, extending a hand.

I shook the offered hand and gasped when the man's eyes flashed silver-white. I'd studied enough in history and mythology books to recognize what that look meant. I pulled my hand back and scooted farther down the bench.

This seem to amuse him. "Oh, don't be shy, Carter."

"But your eyes," I said weakly. "You're a . . . a . . ."

"Vampire? Yes."

"Oh shit," I squeaked. My heart was going a mile a minute. "D-did you make everyone leave the room with — you know, your mind?"

"It took some time, but yes. Those bratty school children were so oblivious that it took a little longer to make them sense danger nearby."

My eyes widened in panic, but he put up a hand. "Don't be frightened. I'm not going to harm you. It's just the easiest way to make people leave. No one lingers in a place where they feel threatened."

"If you're not going to hurt me, then what do you want?"

Alder raised an eyebrow. "Have you ever been fucked against the wall of an Egyptian temple?"

That was the most bizarre pickup line I'd ever heard. I snorted. "Are you serious? Sorry, but I don't hop into bed, or up against a wall, with a man I don't know, let alone a vampire."

"Are you scared of being with a vampire?"

Truth was, I was so turned on by him at that moment that I would have consented to him fucking me in the middle of Times Square, but he *was* a vampire. He was dangerous. Wasn't he? Sitting next to me on that bench, he didn't appear so, but then he smiled and his fangs dropped. His eyes flashed again, and a rush of air escaped my lungs. Lust overwhelmed my senses. I panted with need at the thought of those sharp weapons sinking into my skin.

Alder looked down at the bulge in my pants and laughed softly. "You want this, Carter. You want to feel what it's like for my fangs to pierce your flesh."

"Yes," I mumbled.

Without waiting, he took me by the wrist and pulled me into the temple.

"What if someone sees us?" I asked breathlessly.

"They won't." His fingers caressed my wrist and a calming shudder ran through my body. He sounded so reasonable that I couldn't fight against him. I wasn't sure if he was seducing me, or if I was willing, but I didn't care. I was so hard that I was ready to beg him.

Quickly peeling my shirt over my head, I shoved my shorts and boxers down and began to work on Alder's pants. He unbuttoned his shirt, letting it fall to the floor, and then shoved me against the stone wall.

"So eager." He palmed my ass and lifted me so I wrapped my legs around his waist. It was as though I weighed nothing to him. He held two fingers to my mouth and said, "Get them wet for me."

I whimpered with want, and sucked the digits into my mouth. When they were coated with my spit, Alder reached down and pushed one into my ass. I hissed in pain, but he kept moving, adding another finger and stretching me farther. To distract myself, I plastered my lips over his, thrusting my tongue into his mouth. He spread his fingers apart, scissoring them to stretch me more.

He withdrew from my ass and I felt very empty. The feeling didn't last, though, as he lined up his cock and breeched my ring with a grunt. His large cock rubbed against my prostate, and I bucked.

"Oh, fuck," I moaned.

"You feel amazing," he panted.

The skin of my back scraped painfully against the stone, but I didn't care. The friction of my cock against his hard abs pushed me up to the edge quickly. "C-coming!" I cried.

A loud growl ripped from Alder, and I saw his fangs drop. Terrified excitement gripped me as the sharp teeth sank into my throat. The pain of the bite, and the wet heat of his tongue as he sucked the wound, sent me into the most powerful orgasm I'd ever had. As I felt Alder's cum flood my ass, I covered our stomachs and chests.

"Shit," I muttered, as Alder slowly set me on my feet. "Damn. That was—"

My voice left me when I looked up to see blood dripping down my lover's chin. It brought me back to reality with a vengeance and I freaked.

"Oh no," I said. "Oh, no no no. What did you do? Did you mark me?"

His smile was vicious, but it cleared quickly. "No, my pet.

My bite is invisible once I seal it with my saliva. Didn't you enjoy yourself?"

He gestured toward his cum-covered stomach and I blushed. "It was really good."

"For me as well," he said, wiping his stomach with his undershirt. "I'd like to see you again, if I may."

"Like on a date?" I asked stupidly.

"Yes," he answered, while he finished dressing.

"But you could have anyone. Why me?"

He kissed me, and I closed my eyes, enjoying the sensation. Then I heard his voice in my head. *Your blood calls to me. It is mine. You will love me, Carter.*

"Love you?" I asked in surprise. When I got no response, I opened my eyes and found myself alone. Alder's business card lay at my feet.

"But Carter, you barely know the man," my mother said.

I rolled my eyes. "Mom, it's been four months. He treats me really well. You and Dad will save a ton of money if I move in with Alder."

My father crossed his arms. "It's not about the money, son. I'm just a little hesitant about you moving in with a . . ."

"Member of the undead?" Alder supplied helpfully.

"Not *now*," I told Alder through clenched teeth.

Mom scowled at him. "Would you excuse us so we can talk to our son privately?"

Alder bowed slightly and left the room. I knew he'd listen anyway. My mother continued. "Baby, he's completely controlling you. How do you know he's not using his powers to seduce you?"

I scoffed. "You make him sound like some evil villain."

"But look at you!" Dad snapped. "New hairstyle, new clothes, new car. Everything picked out by Alder, I assume."

Mom sighed. "Carter, sweetie, we're worried about you. You haven't seen any of your friends for weeks. They call us wondering where you are."

"But I love him," I said. At least I thought I did. Alder reminded me daily that I loved him, so after a while I'd started to believe it. I thought about that morning, how roughly he fucked me while he fed from me, and unconsciously rubbed at my neck.

Mom noticed the movement. "How often does he feed from you?"

"Mom! That's none of your business."

"*You are* my business," she said with fire in her eyes. "You are my child, and I will not lose you to him. I know you think you love him, but he's using you. Everyone sees it but you."

"I have to go," I said quietly. Tears filled my eyes as I looked at my mother. "I know you're trying to help, but I'll be okay. I love you, Mom."

She wrapped me in a bone-crushing hug and kissed my cheek. "Just be careful, baby. And if you ever need us, we'll be there. No matter what. You're always welcome here."

"Okay." I hugged my father. "Love you, Dad."

He kissed the top of my head and spoke in a rough voice. "Please call us if you need help, Carter. We love you."

I nodded, and heard Alder clear his throat. My parents said nothing to my boyfriend before we left.

The driver opened the car door for us and I climbed in. Alder fell back against the seat and sighed. "Thank God. I didn't think they'd ever shut up."

"Alder!" I cried. "They're worried about me. And they're my parents. I love them."

"But you love me more?" he asked. The fierce look in his eye made it clear that it wasn't really a question.

I knew better than to argue with him. My arm still hurt from the last time I disagreed with him, so I nodded silently and looked out the window.

Only a month later, I realized what an enormous mistake I'd made. My parents had been right. I was completely under Alder's control, and there was no way to get away from him. If I wasn't with him, I was constantly under the supervision of a bodyguard. I had to ask Alder to use the phone to call my parents. And even then I lied to them and told them how great everything was.

In reality, my life was anything but great. When Alder was in a good mood, he'd seduce me, make love to me, and everything would be wonderful. However, the good moods were coming less and less frequently, and the depth of his rage was growing. I wanted to escape him. But whenever I'd talk about taking a break from our relationship, he'd mention my family, and how he'd like to spend some time with them. It was an outright threat—I wasn't about to put them in jeopardy. So instead, I suffered in silence.

One night, Alder said someone was coming by after dinner. No one ever came to the apartment, so I was stunned. Excitement made my heart race as I took my shower and dressed. I couldn't wait to see who it was.

At seven o'clock, the doorbell rang. I remained in the kitchen while Alder went to the foyer to answer the door.

"Ah," Alder said. "So good to see you."

There was a pause. "Of course."

The voice was smooth and low, the opposite of Alder's scratchy tenor. The sound did something to me that made me blush.

Alder spoke again. "Come and meet my boyfriend."

"*Boyfriend?*" the visitor asked. He seemed surprised.

Footsteps grew closer until Alder entered the room, followed by the most handsome man I'd ever seen in my life. The similarity of the facial features was striking, but this man was taller than Alder, and had light blond hair.

I stared until Alder wrapped his arm around my waist and drew me to his side. "This is Carter. Carter, say hello to my brother Freyr."

The expression on Freyr's face was hard to read. He seemed almost afraid. He tentatively took my hand. "It's nice to meet you."

I couldn't form an answer. I was too busy trying to figure out why it felt like lightning had traveled directly from Freyr's fingers and into my heart.

Chapter Two—Freyr

Standing there, holding Carter's hand, my world changed. The rightness of his fingers grasping mine made my heart soar. I knew, though, that with Alder standing there, I had to remain calm. I couldn't give away my instant attraction to my brother's boyfriend. That would've been a fatal mistake, for me as well as Carter.

I pulled my hand away and turned back to Alder. "So why the invitation? Couldn't our lawyers have handled the paperwork?"

Alder feigned surprise. "Now what's wrong with me wanting a visit from my baby brother?"

"Besides the fact that we haven't seen each other in years? Nothing, I suppose."

Carter was still staring at me, mouth slightly open, and I saw Alder raise an eyebrow at him. I had to defuse the situation, so I strode into the living room and dropped into a leather chair that faced the kitchen. "Could I have a drink? It was a long trip."

My request seemed to snap Carter out of his trance. "Oh! Yes, I'm sorry." He put a slim hand on Alder's arm and asked, "Would you like a drink, honey?"

The affectionate tone seemed to please my brother. He wrapped a hand around the back of Carter's neck and pulled him in for an intense kiss. I knew it was Alder's way of marking his property in front of me, so I looked away.

When he let Carter go, he said, "I'll have Scotch. You may have water."

I bristled at Alder's domineering attitude. Carter smiled weakly at me. "What will you have, Freyr?"

"I'll have water, too, please."

Carter brought me a glass, and I accepted it, careful not to let our fingers touch. Then I went back to studiously ignoring him. "So why buy me out now, Alder? There's nothing left of the building."

Alder took the glass from Carter and pulled him down onto his lap. "True, but I'm thinking of building a new house on the site."

I shook my head. Why he would want to live anywhere near where our family had been murdered centuries ago was beyond me. "Fine. I have no desire to ever go back there anyway, so it's yours."

"Go back where?" Carter asked timidly. Alder glared at him, as though he wasn't allowed to talk without permission. I saw Alder's fingers tighten around his arm. The young man winced. "I-I'm sorry, Alder. I didn't mean to interfere."

If I didn't get out of that apartment soon, I knew I was going to do something drastic. I drained my glass and stood. "Well, we've had our drink, and you've got what you wanted. I've a lot more important things to do with my time."

"Come visit again soon, brother," Alder laughed. He didn't get up, holding Carter down with a firm hand on his shoulder.

"Goodbye," Carter added.

"Yeah. Bye." Before I left, I risked one more look back, and my heart ached. Desolation filled me as my gaze met Carter's. Helplessness shone in those bright blue eyes, and there was nothing I could do. I closed the door and walked away, leaving a piece of me behind in Alder's hands.

I was glad Alder had extended an invitation for me to visit more frequently. I took him up on the offer. I hoped that somehow fate would intervene, and I'd be able to take Carter away. Until then, I'd do my best to make him feel less alone. The more I saw of him, though, the worse he seemed. As time went on, I witnessed Alder's hold on him began to strip the humanity from the man I knew was fated to be my mate. Something had to be done before he became a soulless hand puppet who functioned only at his master's bidding. I'd seen it happen time and again for hundreds of years. Alder played with men — feeding on them, healing them, then feeding on them again — until they were empty shells — still human, but their minds were dead. When he tired of his toys, Alder usually gave the near-dead men to his immortal servants. The meals were much appreciated.

My throat constricted at the thought of Carter suffering such a horrible fate. I decided to take him away before he was destroyed. Of course, if Alder discovered us, it would be a fight to the death, but I couldn't take it anymore. I drove to Alder's house that night.

Carter was alone. "Hey, Freyr," he called blandly as he flipped through TV channels.

I went to sit by him on the sofa. "How are you?"

"Fine, I guess. I'm glad Alder's gone for a few days."

"Oh really?" My heart skipped. Maybe this would be the night we could get away.

He nodded and bit his lip shyly. "I'm really happy to see you."

I stumbled over my words. "Happy to see *me?*"

"I'm always happy to see you. You're nice, kind. I feel safe with you." He blushed and turned toward me. His nervous smile filled my heart to bursting. The thought gave me the courage to go forward with my seduction. I didn't have to seduce him, however. Carter leaned in and kissed me.

I pushed him up by his shoulders and asked, "Are you sure about this? It's very dangerous to defy Alder."

"It doesn't matter, Freyr. My feelings are too strong to ignore. Please."

The simple plea was my undoing. I pulled him toward one of the empty rooms in the far wing of the house where the guards outside wouldn't hear. We slowly undressed, and I fell to my knees to worship his perfection.

"You are so beautiful. This body —"

I stopped and reeled back. My eyes widened in horror at the bite marks covering the inside of Carter's legs. Some of them were very recent, still angry and pink.

Carter twisted from my grip, sobbing. "It was my fault. I didn't listen to him. I deserved it."

My heart broke, and I clutched his trembling body to my own. "You never deserved this. Let me love and heal you. I'll show you what it means to be truly adored."

His hands brushed through my hair, and I looked up at him. Though his eyes were still wet with tears, he smiled. "I love you, Freyr. I always have."

If I could have cried, I would have sobbed with relief at his declaration. I ran my tongue up his dick from the base to the tip and swallowed his length in one swift movement. He collapsed back so he was half-sitting on the bed. His reaction was so intense that my own cock throbbed to the point of bursting. As much as I wanted to give him the ultimate pleasure, I knew we might not have much time together.

If Alder feels Carter's mood change . . .

No. I pushed the thought out of my mind and concentrated on the writhing form beneath me. With gentle kisses and quick flicks of my tongue, I worked my way up his body. I lowered down onto him so our cocks rubbed together.

"Oh fuck." he said, eyes rolling back in his head. "I've wanted this for so long. Make love to me, Freyr."

Sweeter words I'd never heard. I pushed his legs up, and he caught them behind his knees and held them. His perfect ass was open for me, and I leaned over to enjoy it. I lowered my mouth to his balls. I sucked one into my mouth and he was whimpering and writhing in seconds. I then feathered my tongue across his hole, and the quiet mews of pleasure became cries of ecstasy. "Holy shit! Yes, oh, fuck. That feels . . . don't stop."

"I love the taste of you, Carter. The way you move is more than I can stand. I must have you right now." He nodded frantically, so I wet my finger in my mouth, then slid it slowly into him. He wasn't a virgin, so it wasn't strictly necessary to take such care before we made love, but I wanted him to relish the moment. A second finger slid in easily and I rubbed them against the sensitive spot within.

"Fuck! Hang on." He ran out of the room and was back in seconds with a bottle of lubed. He tossed it to me and said, "Here. Get inside me!"

"With pleasure." I slicked my cock and slid into the welcoming hole. To finally be inside him after all that time was too much. I thrust hard and grunted with every stroke. "I . . . love you, Carter."

He began to shake with excitement. "I love you too." I wrapped a hand around his cock and he came hard, covering his belly. The contractions of his muscles pushed me over the edge and I cried out. My hot cum filled him as my cock spasmed.

"So good," he moaned. Before I could stop him, he sat up and grabbed my bottom lip between his teeth. He bit hard enough to break the skin, and when my blood touched his tongue, his eyes glazed over. Only a small drop of a vampire's blood was enough to awaken a human's craving. Carter bit harder and sucked at my lip. I wasn't sure if he'd never tasted Alder's blood before, so when he tasted mine, his body reacted with a crazed need.

When a human feeds from a vampire, it's a powerful, sexual experience. Since Alder had consumed Carter's blood, the immortal would be able to sense changes in the human's mood and heart. Now that Carter had made love with me, and had such a reaction to me, I knew Alder would certainly discover what we'd done, I had to stop him.

"No!" I cried, pushing him away. "Oh, God, Carter. What have you done?"

He strained to reach my mouth again. "Please, Freyr. It's so good. I want more." When I wouldn't let him near my face, he surprised me by grabbing my wrist and biting. "*Mmm*," he sighed as he licked the wound.

I pushed him back and stared in horror at my blood on his chin. "Carter, listen. Alder is very powerful, more so than me or any other vampire. Once he took your blood, he was able to plant a piece of himself inside you. Now he feels your heart, your mind. When we made love, he felt it."

"He felt us having sex? Oh, shit. That means—he'll come after you!" He pushed against my shoulders, trying to free himself. "Let me go. You've got to leave, Freyr."

"What? No. You're coming with me!"

He shook his head. "I can't. He keeps guards around my family all the time. He's made it clear that he'll kill them if I try to leave. I'm begging you, Freyr. If you love me, then go."

I was desperate. "But Carter, if he takes you away, we might never see each other again!"

"Please, *leave*," he begged. "At least I'll know you're alive."

Reluctantly, I pulled my clothes on. I kissed him once more. "I'll always love you, Carter."

"I love you too," he sobbed.

One last kiss and I left, calling to him. "I'll find you. Wherever he takes you. I'll never stop looking. We'll be together someday."

Chapter Three—Carter

As soon as Freyr left, I took a shower, scrubbing furiously to eradicate any trace of my lover from my body. My skin pink and raw, I slipped into pajamas and went to bed. My body wouldn't stop shaking. At any moment, Alder would return, and I resigned myself to death.

Near dawn, I awoke to a deafening crash. I jumped up from the bed to find Alder hovering in the splintered doorway. A wild look crossed his face, and his eyes lit with anger. I shrank back, but not fast enough to avoid a backhand slap to my jaw. It wasn't the first time he'd struck me, but it was the first time I feared for my life.

"Wait, Alder."

His fist connected with my cheek, knocking me to the floor. "You reek of his scent! Did you think I wouldn't know?"

Another slap split my lip and I mumbled around the blood. "It wasn't—"

He crouched next to me and hissed in my ear. "Did you like it when he fucked you? How did he convince you to do it? Did he lie to you and tell you how beautiful you are? Maybe he told you he loved you? Answer me!"

His foot connected with my ribs. I cried out and attempted to drag myself away, but he took me by the hair and pulled me to my feet.

I begged him, "Please. It meant nothing."

"Liar! I could feel the heat in your blood, and the pulse of your veins while he drove into you."

He pushed me face down on the bed and straddled my

legs. When I felt cold hands at my waist, I screamed, "No! You can't do this."

"Silence! You must be punished for your infidelity, Carter." He used my belt to bind my hands behind my back. When I twisted to free myself, pain shot through my wrists. He laughed. "Oh, come now. Surely you don't think you will escape? Keep struggling, though. The movement will make your ass contract beautifully. Pardon me for not preparing you properly, pet, but I must make haste to find your lover and deal with him accordingly. He will pay for this betrayal."

I moaned in anguish. "No, please, Alder. I'll give my life if you spare his. You can torture me for eternity and I will never say his name again. I'm begging you."

"How very noble," he sneered, "but you mistake my meaning, pet. I'm not going to kill your lover." Relief washed over me, but it didn't last. The vampire laughed. "That way, I can watch him suffer after I lay your body at his feet."

Cold, hard dread paralyzed me. Bile churned in my stomach, and I stopped struggling. He gripped my hips with bruising strength. I cried out in pain. The last thing I remembered was begging for mercy before his fangs sank into my throat.

Alder was speaking rapidly into his cell phone when I woke. The conversation was in German, so I had no clue what he said. He sat on the side of the bed, and I noticed he wasn't wearing any clothes. His smooth, slender body reflected the morning sun as though it was a white rock on the beach. It would have been beautiful, had it not concealed such an evil soul.

I turned from Alder, and pain shot through my legs and butt. I was undressed as well, and the aches reminded me of the night before. I'd lost track of the number of times Alder had bitten me, and the thought of the animalistic way he took me, over and over, made my stomach cramp. Gagging on suppressed bile, I stood up to go to the bathroom, but Alder took hold of my wrist. The phone call ended abruptly, and he yanked me back onto the bed.

"Where do you think you're going?"

"I need to use the bathroom."

"You have five minutes. Then come to the kitchen."

I scrambled into the tiled room and stood under the shower, trying to wash the smell of him off me. Sadness overcame me, and I silently called to Freyr. I wondered where he was, and if I would ever see him again. Would Alder make good on his threat to kill me and deliver my body to my lover?

All too quickly, my five minutes were up. I dressed and hurried to the kitchen. My tormentor was preparing a plate of food, with his back to me. Without turning, he said, "Sit."

I did as he commanded, and winced at the sting from my ass. Very carefully, I asked, "Could I please take some ibuprofen?"

With a disgusted sigh, he nodded. I got a glass of water and pulled the bottle of pills off the shelf. For a moment, I thought about swallowing all of the small brown pills, but I wasn't sure if it would be fatal, so I just took four.

I didn't dare look at Alder, and returned to my seat silently. He slid my meal toward me, and my stomach turned. It was steak, nearly raw, with a puddle of blood gathering around the edge of the plate.

When I didn't move, he handed me a fork and steak knife and sneered. "That knife would do nothing to me, so don't bother."

"This is *breakfast?*" I asked in horror. "I'm not eating that."

"You need iron for the blood loss," Alder replied with an evil smile. I pushed my lips together into a straight line and shook my head. His expression changed in a Jekyll-and-Hyde fashion and he roared, "Then you get nothing!" He grabbed the plate and hurled it across the room. A grotesque mess of shattered pottery, steak, and blood slid down the wall.

He wrapped me too tightly in his arms and sighed wearily. "Oh, Carter. I have tried so hard to be patient with you." Suddenly, he pushed me toward the couch and I fell over it, banging my knee painfully on the glass coffee table. Ignoring my yelp of pain, he jerked my body up so I was sitting in his lap — a grim parody of a child with Santa. He stroked my jaw with the backs of his fingers then continued, with feigned concern. "What am I to do, pet? I'm trying to help you, and perhaps give you a second chance, but as you insist on defying me . . ."

With a malicious chuckle, he took my wrist and bit down hard. I cried out in pain, and stared at him with wide eyes. After saying a prayer for a quick death, my heart called out once more to Freyr, *"I love you. I'm sorry."*

But Alder wasn't finished with me. Instead of death, I suffered something much worse. Without bothering to close the bleeding wound on my wrist, he gathered his phone and briefcase and pulled on his coat.

"I'll be back later."

When he was gone, I stumbled to the sink and tried to wash out the bite, but vampire bites did not close on their own. The only cure was their venomous saliva. I got an idea of calling one of the other vampires I knew, I wasn't allowed to have a phone. A quick check revealed that the door was also bolted from the outside.

I had no escape. My head began to pound from pain and the sheer terror of the situation. A few crackers were the only food left in the kitchen, and after I ate those, my stomach began to rebel. I lay back down on the couch and wished for death.

Weeks and then months went by, and still I was trapped in the hell of Alder's wrath. We'd moved to yet another of his houses, and since he blindfolded me during the drive, I had no idea where I was, or even if I was still in New York. He didn't bite me every day. Some days he acted as if nothing was wrong and treated me as any boyfriend would. I ate what I wanted, and I was allowed to watch TV. Other days, however, his demon surfaced, and he would nearly drain me before locking me in a darkened room. As the winter months closed in, we moved again, and I gave up all hope of ever seeing Freyr.

During one of his rages, Alder bit fiercely into my wrist. I didn't react to the pain. I'd become immune to it. That day was different, however. He licked his lips and said, "You know, pet, I haven't seen your family in a long time. I think I'll call on them right now. Pity you'll never get the chance again."

Knowing he meant to kill them, I cried, "Why, Alder? Why are you doing this?"

He went to the door, turned, and grinned. "Because I can."

The lights went off, and I was plunged into darkness. Blood from my wrist began to seep through my sleeve. It felt slimy against my skin. What could I do? Absolutely nothing. For hours, I cried for my family, hoping Alder wouldn't make them suffer. Grief finally, mercifully, overcame consciousness.

"Carter, wake up."

Bright sunlight burned my eyes. I was on the couch. The wound on my wrist was closed. Alder sat on the chair opposite me, smiling like a snake.

He took in a deep, satisfied breath. "They were very nice, your family." A shuddering sob went through me and Alder's smile widened. "Oh, pet, don't cry. I brought you something, to help you feel better."

"What is it?" I asked.

With a dramatic sweep of his arm, he brought a teddy bear

out from behind his back. I recognized it as belonging to my eight-year-old brother, Jacob. Horror stole my breath when I saw the large splatter of blood on its head. I leaned over the arm of the couch and vomited onto the carpet.

"He was cute," the devil incarnate said. "So was your sister. How old was Lidell, anyway? Oh, right! She was sixteen. It's too bad they had to see your parents die, but I had to deal with the bigger threat first. Besides, children are much sweeter, so I wanted to save the best for last."

Every shred of love and hope was ripped from my heart. My soul keened as it shriveled.

Now, he couldn't hurt me any more than he already had— my anger switched on and I decided to fight. I ran to the kitchen and grabbed a steak knife out of the drawer. I held it out and screamed, "Fuck you! I don't care what you do to me. Your brother will find you and send you to Hell."

Alder chuckled. "I've told you before that a pitiful steak knife is no match for me."

Where I found the courage to do it, I'll never know, but I smiled back at him and said, "I know that." Before he could stop me, I dragged the blade across my throat.

Chapter Four—Carter

Ten Months Later

"Wait, Alder."

His fist connected with my cheek, knocking me to the floor. "You reek of his scent! Did you think I wouldn't know?"

Another slap split my lip and I mumbled around the blood. "It wasn't — "

He crouched next to me and hissed in my ear. "Did you like it when he fucked you? How did he convince you to do it? Did he lie to you and tell you how beautiful you are? Maybe he told you he loved you? Answer me!"

His foot connected with my ribs. I cried out and attempted to drag myself away, but he took me by the hair and pulled me to my feet.

"Please. It meant nothing."

"Liar! I could feel the heat in your blood, and the pulse of your veins while he drove into you."

He pushed me face down on the bed and straddled my legs. When I felt cold hands at my waist, I screamed, "No! You can't do this."

"Silence! You must be punished for your infidelity, Carter." He bound my hands behind my back. When I twisted to free myself, pain shot through my wrists. He laughed. "Oh, come now. Surely you don't think you will escape? Keep struggling, though. The movement will make your ass contract beautifully. Pardon me for not preparing you, my sweet one, but I must make haste to find your lover and deal with him accordingly. He will pay for this betrayal."

I moaned in anguish. "No, please, Alder. I'll give my life if you spare his. You can torture me for eternity and I will never say his *name again. I'm begging you."*

"How very noble," he sneered, "but you mistake my meaning, pet. I'm not going to kill your lover." Relief washed over me, but it didn't last. The vampire laughed. "That way, I can watch him suffer after I lay your body at his feet."

Cold, hard dread paralyzed me. Bile churned in my stomach, and I stopped struggling. He gripped my hips with bruising strength. I cried out in pain. The last thing I remembered was begging for mercy before his fangs sank into my throat.

I gasped at the pain in my head when I woke from my nightmare. I looked around the room in which I lay, and my mouth fell open in shock. I could see everything—silvery flecks of dust swirling around the air vent in the ceiling; a fingerprint on the window; each individual thread in my warm blanket. Instinctively, I sniffed and grimaced. The odors of antibacterial soap and industrial cleaner stung my nose.

The air was dry, and I licked my lips. When my tongue caught on something sharp, I touched the tip of my finger to my canine tooth. I yelped in pain and examined my finger. A bead of blood collected on the puncture. I licked it off and watched as the wound magically closed and disappeared.

I had become a vampire. The revelation was more than my foggy mind could comprehend. I remembered nothing of what had happened. My head swam with confusion. I whimpered and sobbed, but no tears came to my eyes.

The door to my room flew open, and a tall, blond man rushed to my bedside. For a moment, I thought he was the monster from my nightmare, but his gaze met mine and my panic lessened. He looked familiar, but my brain was overloaded and I couldn't focus. A lock of blond hair fell across his brow, and he smiled warmly. His voice was soothing. "Calm yourself, Carter. It's all right. It's me, Freyr."

"Freyr?" My voice was a garbled croak.

"Yes, it's me, baby."

"Where am I?"

"This is Kernborn, a private clinic for vampires and humans alike. What do you remember?"

Flashes of memory flitted through my head. The vision of the blade scraping across my skin made me shiver violently. Then I remembered the blood-soaked teddy bear.

"Jake!" I cried. "Oh my God, my family! Where's Alder?"

Freyr's strong hand held me down in the bed. "He's not here, Carter. I'll explain everything."

"But . . . how am I alive?" I rubbed a hand over my neck and cringed at the memory of slitting my own throat.

Freyr drew a shuddering breath and kissed my forehead. "As I told you then, I never stopped looking for you. Alder isn't the only one with connections. Don't forget I am also a von Drubich."

With a shiver, I replied, "Trust me, I won't."

He scowled, but otherwise ignored the implied criticism. "Right after I left you that night, I was able to convince one of Alder's servants to keep me informed of his movements. Then I had Stefan, one of my oldest friends, follow my brother as he moved from house to house. We never lost track of you, but it was impossible to get close enough. Alder had you so well-guarded not even I could have freed you. His men were on orders to kill you if anyone but Alder came near the house. Then one night . . ."

It didn't take much to understand. I looked away and said, "He killed my family."

Freyr swallowed hard. "The servant didn't know what was happening until Alder had already left, so by the time we arrived at your family's home, it was too late for your parents and sister."

A spark of recognition lit in my numbed brain. "What about my brother?" I asked. "What happened to him?"

Freyr took my hands in his and looked me straight in the

eye. "Your brother was still alive when we got to him, but barely. He'd been strangled and bitten several times. Apparently Alder left him, thinking he would die."

"But he didn't?" I guessed. "So where is he?"

Freyr had to clear his throat before he said, "There had been too much oxygen deprivation, and Jacob was unresponsive when we arrived. We transferred him here to the clinic as quickly as we could, then we raced to my brother's house. I was afraid when you learned of what had happened, the grief would be too much for you."

"It was. I can't believe I tried to . . . how did I live through that?"

"Again, Alder was too confident in himself. He had no idea Stefan and I were so close, so when you injured yourself, he simply assumed you would die. He left for another of his houses, and I let him go. My first priority was you. When we found you, you were unconscious and near death."

"You changed me," I stated.

"Not I," he said.

I couldn't believe it. "Who did it, then? Why didn't you? I wanted it to be you!"

"Shh," he cooed. "When a vampire turns someone, it doesn't mean the new vampire becomes a . . . slave or anything. We don't claim ownership of newborns. It was Stefan who turned you, and it was for a very good reason."

"What reason?"

He ran a finger along my lip. "Because I wanted you as a mate, but I wanted that to be your decision. You'd already tasted my blood. If I had turned you, and tasted yours, we would have been mated without your consent. I couldn't do that."

Horror struck me and I gasped. "Does that mean I'm mated to Alder?"

"No, my love. You never tasted his blood. Each needs the

other's blood to join as mates."

Sweet relief washed over me. "Oh, thank God! But . . ."

"What is it?"

"Is what happened to my brother the reason I was drugged for so long?"

"Yes. By the time we could move you to the hospital, Jacob was on life support. I wanted you to make the decision to take him off the ventilator, but after you'd finished your transition, and we brought you to see him, you went into a rage. Alder had severely injured your brother, and the sight of his little broken body made your beast lash out with a ferocity I'd never seen in one so young."

The thought horrified me. "What did I do? Did I kill someone?"

"No, but it was very close. I made the decision to sedate you."

"How did you sedate me? I don't get it."

"Your blood is very powerful. When a human consumes a vampire's blood in small quantities, it produces an intense high, a sense of euphoria. In larger doses, the human will of course become immortal. If a *vampire* drinks his own blood, in small quantities, he will feel the same high as a human. However, if a vampire drinks a lot of his own blood, it will . . . put him to sleep—essentially a coma."

I nodded woodenly. "So you put me into a coma?"

"Yes. I hoped the time would allow your mind and heart to heal. I couldn't risk letting you wake until you were able to handle all that had happened."

"But Jake!" I cried. "He was all alone. I could have been with him."

"You were with him," Freyr said. "Your brother was in this same room for the entire nine months he lived. Last month, he contracted pneumonia and we knew he would not survive. We ended his life support and I moved him into your bed. He died in your arms."

If I could have cried, I would have. I would have sobbed and roared and bawled and let the tears pour down, but all I could do was curl into a ball on my bed and endure the heart-wrenching grief. Freyr lay down behind me, tentatively placing his hand on my side. I grabbed his arm and pulled it tight around me, securing myself to him. He kissed the back of my neck and we slept.

We had not slept long before there was a knock on the door. A young, attractive human nurse came into the room. "All right, Freyr, I think it's—oh, I'm . . . I didn't mean to . . ."

Freyr chuckled. "It's all right, Katherine. Just taking a little nap."

"Is that what they call it these days?" She attached a blood pressure cuff to my arm. "Well, he is beautiful, I have to give you that."

"That he is. He's the most beautiful being I have ever known."

She removed the cuff and stowed it in her pocket. "Pressure's a bit low. Have you fed yet, sweet thing?" I assumed she was talking to me, and I shook my head. She rolled her eyes. "Freyr, you said you'd do it yourself. Should I get the transfuser?"

That got a stronger response. "No, no," he said quickly. "Right now. I'll do it now."

"You'd better." She flicked off the overhead light and said, "A little mood lighting might help."

"Out!" Freyr barked. When she was gone, he pulled me closer against him and whispered in my ear, "Take my blood, Carter."

He held his wrist to my mouth and my fangs lengthened. I bit down as though I'd been doing it all my life, and it was like biting into a cherry. A quick pop through the skin was followed by an intense rush of sweet, thick liquid that was instantly addictive. After I tuned out my own reaction, I heard Freyr behind me, crying in ecstasy.

"Oh, shit, Carter. I've waited so long for this."

I sucked hard and swallowed a mouthful, then another, and another until Freyr pulled his wrist away. "You'll be the death of me if you keep up like that. Here, close the wound."

A tantalizing drop had collected on his wrist, and I sucked at it quickly. Then I slicked my tongue over the puncture wounds and watched them close. I turned to look sheepishly at Freyr. "Sorry."

"Absolutely nothing to be sorry for," Freyr said. "This has been an emotional day for you, and your body will need a lot of nourishment for a while."

We snuggled together for a while, and I never wanted to get up, but something was keeping me from rest. He asked what was wrong and I answered, "My family. Maybe it's because of the coma, but I'm having a hard time remembering them."

Freyr cleared his throat and stroked my arm. "If you would like, I can help you remember."

"How?" I said skeptically.

He retrieved a syringe filled with blood from the table next to my bed. "This will heighten your feelings, and let you focus on the fond memories of your family."

"What on earth is it?"

"It's your blood," Freyr said quickly, as if I wouldn't catch onto the fact that he was about to inject me with a vampire equivalent of ecstasy.

"No way. Fuck that shit. You're not putting me out again."

He sighed in defeat. "Carter, this is only enough to calm your mind and allow you to concentrate. Please believe me when I say the effect will be temporary. I'm trying to make it easier, my love."

There was a genuine concern in his eyes, a truthfulness I couldn't ignore. "All right. Do it."

Without giving me time to change my mind, he sank the needle into a vein in my elbow. A rush of cold, followed by a soothing heat, raced to my mind. "Oh, shit," I muttered. "That's . . . fuck, that's good."

Freyr smoothed the hair from my forehead and whispered, "Think of Lidell, Carter. Think of your brother, Jacob, and your parents." I nodded and lay back on the bed, letting my blood fool my senses.

I sat in the back yard of a large white house, trying to read a book, but two children kept interrupting me. My brother Jacob ran around Lidell while she held a ball out of his reach. My mother stood up from the picnic table and put a hand over her eyes to see past the sun's glare. I looked like her, with dark hair and a long, slim body. She called, "Jacob! Lidell! Come over and finish your lunch."

Jacob ran over to the table and gulped down a glass of juice, letting it dribble over his chin. "Quit it," Lidell said. "God, you're so gross. Dad, will you tell him to stop being so disgusting?"

Our father was the opposite of my mother: blond, muscular, and blue-eyed. He settled the petty feud between my siblings with a few stern words and then walked over to me. With a shake of his head, he asked, "Do you think they'll ever stop arguing?"

"Probably not," my younger self said. "They'll probably go to the grave bickering."

He laughed and clapped me on the shoulder. "Have you finished packing?"

"Just about. I can't believe I'm starting college next week. Is Mom getting used to the idea?"

"You know your mother," he said with a raised eyebrow. "She'll cry and beg you to stay."

"Brooklyn's not that far away, Dad. She can visit."

"Well, I'm sure she'll be down there within a month, so keep your apartment clean."

The images began to fade, and a dull, empty sensation thumped at my chest. The same cold rush I'd felt initially passed through my system, and I woke with a quiet gasp. An arm around my waist prevented me from moving far. I craned my neck around and saw Freyr's blond head tucked into a pillow behind me, and the emptiness was filled with a yearning for the beautiful immortal. I turned my whole body in his grasp and ran my tongue lightly across his plump bottom lip.

His beautiful blue eyes opened, and the corners wrinkled with a smile. "Mm. Welcome back, my love. Did it work?"

I wrapped my arms around his neck. "Yes. I remembered the weekend before I moved to Brooklyn. We had a picnic in the back yard. It was wonderful."

"I'm so glad," Freyr said. "Speaking of moving, are you ready to go home?"

I was shocked. "With you?"

He looked nervous. "Yes?"

The shy vulnerability tugged at my heart. With a quiet moan, I pulled his face to mine and explored the inside of his mouth with my tongue. While I tasted him, I rubbed my hand lightly over the large bulge in his pants and whispered, "Take me home."

"Oh, fuck," Freyr said, licking the wet kisses from his lips. "I think my cock is too hard to drive."

The drive was long and silent, but our lusty glances and heavy breathing — not to mention the way we both kept adjusting our pants around rock-hard erections — spoke volumes. After half an hour, it was unbearable. My dick felt like it was being pierced with a red-hot poker. My balls drew up so tight it brought tears to my eyes, and I couldn't figure out why I was quite so hard. Then it occurred to me that I'd gone ten months without sex.

That did it.

"I'm sorry, but . . . Ican'tstanditanymore." I knew even if I came twice right then, it still wouldn't be a problem getting it up again when we got home. I unzipped my pants and pulled my cock out, smearing pre-come around the tip and over my hand.

Freyr jerked the wheel, but then recovered as he snuck peeks at my show, licking his lips and smiling. "You torture me, my love."

There were no long, slow strokes, as in foreplay. It was quick and rough, and I screwed my eyes up against the painful pleasure. Within minutes, I came hard, accompanied by a loud, long groan, trying to catch the blasts with my hand. My strokes slowed, and I stared at the cum that covered my hands . . . and the dashboard.

I grimaced. "Sorry, Freyr. I didn't —"

His gaze was locked on my hand, which loosely cradled my dick. He pulled off the road and slammed on the brakes. With trembling fingers, he took my wrist and dragged the flat of his tongue through my cum. If the act was intense for me, it must have been mind-blowing for Freyr. His grip on my wrist tightened, and he worked his tongue over my hand as if he was starving, gently nipping, then sucking my fingers hard.

It was the most erotic thing I'd ever witnessed. I wondered if it was like drinking my blood in a way. "Do I taste good, Freyr?"

"Mmmhmm," he grunted around my thumb. His free hand went down and wrapped around my dick, which hadn't gone down at all.

"Fuck, yes," I moaned. "Bite me. Take my blood."

Sighing miserably, he sat up. "I'm sorry, but no."

My erection fizzled. "Why not?"

He gripped my chin in his hand and brought my face

within inches of his own. "Because when I sink my fangs into that sweet skin and let your blood flow onto my tongue, I plan on having my cock so far up your ass you'll be nearly insane with pleasure. When I take you as my mate, I want you screaming my name."

My jaw slackened. He let go, and pulled back onto the road.

CHAPTER FIVE—CARTER

A high wall surrounded the Amsel estate. A monitored gate stood at the edge of the huge property. Several vampires walked along the top of the wall, scanning the surrounding forest.

"Expecting someone?" I asked.

Freyr's expression was deadly serious as he pulled up to the gate. "I am always expecting someone."

He opened the black-tinted window of the Jaguar just enough for the guard to see his eyes. The man inclined his head slightly. "Guten Abend, mein Herr." Then he stooped over a little more and addressed me. "Wilkommen, Herr Denwright—"

Freyr cut him off with a raised hand. "In English, Jonas. Mr. Denwright doesn't speak German."

"I am sorry." He spoke with a thick accent. "Welcome, Herr Denwright."

I chuckled. Freyr rolled his eyes. "Has anyone been seen?"

The guard swallowed nervously. "Nein, aber Stefan wartet auf Sie im—"

"English," Freyr reminded him sternly.

Jonas snapped to attention and stammered a second apology. "I-I-I'm sorry, mein—Mr. Amsel. There has been no activity. Stefan waits for you in the office."

"Fine. Call him and tell him I'm here." He looked at me and smiled, but it wasn't at all convincing.

When he continued down the driveway, I said, "Talk to me, Freyr. You're worried."

"Of course I'm worried. If anyone comes near you, they're going to pay dearly."

I narrowed my eyes. "I'm not made of glass. Do you think I'm completely incapable of taking care of myself?"

We pulled up to the door and he turned to face me. "Carter, you've just woken after ten months. There are many things you need to learn. I want you to be prepared should anything happen."

I smiled nervously. "I didn't think of that. Do I get to meet everyone tonight?"

Freyr rubbed his hand over my thigh slowly and said, "Tomorrow, my love. Tonight is for us." There was so much promise in his words my stomach twisted with lust. He kissed me gently. "Welcome home."

The limestone walls of the enormous mansion burned pink and gold in the fading sun. The lines of the building were simple, without the forbidding crenellations and turrets of a medieval structure. Inside, the front hall was very large. Dark timbers stretched across the ceiling and down the rough, plastered walls.

In the center of the room stood several men. I guess their ages varied from late teens to well past fifty. I could tell by their scent they were all vampires.

"Good evening, sir," said one gentleman. He seemed to be the oldest of the group, maybe fifty human years. His gray hair showed a few signs of the rich brown it had once been, and laugh lines around his eyes highlighted the bright blue of his irises. He took Freyr's coat, then held his hand out for my jacket. I awkwardly slipped it off. It fell to the floor, and the man, who seemed to be a butler of sorts, leaned down to retrieve it.

I snatched it up. "Got it, thanks."

The overeager man straightened and glanced at Freyr nervously, as though they were breaking some holy commandment by letting me pick up after myself. Freyr looked at me and smirked.

The man's wide smile returned and he said, "We're so glad to have you here at last, Mr. Denwright. My name is Lowner. If you need anything at all, just ask."

"Okay," I said lamely.

Another one of the staff stepped forward to greet me, but Freyr took my hand. "He'll meet you all tomorrow. He needs rest."

They all nodded as Freyr whipped me up the stairs. Halfway up, the stairs split off to the left and right. We took the latter route. When we reached the door at the end of the hall, Freyr suddenly appeared shy.

"I hope you like it," he told me shyly.

"I'm sure I will." I turned the knob and pushed the heavy oak door open.

The room was very large, but with low ceilings. Three windows pierced the south wall. Long, gauzy curtains billowed on the light breeze. I thought it was unusually warm for May, then I remembered that, except for extreme heat waves or subzero freezes, a change in air temperature meant very little to a vampire. I smiled to myself and continued to explore.

The floors had once been painted a dark color, but lines of bare wood traced where feet had walked for centuries: door to bed, bed to window, window to door, and so on. The walls were the same dark timber and white plaster as the hall. The fireplace was surrounded by very old blue-and-white decorative tiles. On the mantle was a picture of me in a simple, black frame. Next to that, in a larger frame, was a picture of my family.

I ran my fingers over their faces. "Thank you, Freyr."

He seemed relieved. "So you like the room?"

"I love it." I threw my arms around his neck.

"Excellent. This will be your room. Mine is next door."

"*My* room?" I asked with a desolate feeling in my gut. I frowned. Letting my arms fall to my sides, I said, "But I thought we—"

"I didn't want to assume anything, in case you needed some time to get used to the idea."

I grabbed his hand and rubbed my dick with it. He cupped my balls with his fingers while the heel of his hand pressed on the curve of my shaft. Freyr's eyes widened when he felt the bulge. I said, "Feel this? *This* has just awakened after ten fucking months. *This* is twitching at the thought of you up my ass. *This* does not want a room of its own."

"Oh, fuck." He brought me down hard onto the floor and lay above me, grinning. His tongue pressed deep into the hollow of my throat, and I strained my hips up to meet his. Before I had even unbuttoned his pants, though, a voice came from the doorway.

"Ahem."

"Go away," Freyr snapped. The command was accompanied by a low growl.

"You still think you can scare me after all these years?"

Freyr rested his head on my shoulder in defeat, and pushed himself up. I rose and stood behind him, willing my dick to calm down. When I looked around Freyr, I saw what appeared to be a giant standing on the threshold. The vampire must have been over six and a half feet tall, with broad shoulders and a narrow waist. His bright blond hair glowed in the light from the hall.

The apparition smiled and said, "He's got my good looks, Frey."

"Let's hope not," Freyr said. He turned to me. "Carter, this is Stefan."

So this was my creator. He was nothing like I'd expected. I offered my hand, which was swallowed in his large paw.

"Hello," I said timidly.

"How are you, Carter? Sick of my friend's ugly face yet?" His fingers tightened around mine and I felt a slight caress. Instantly, Freyr stood between us, growling.

"Back away from my mate," he demanded.

Stefan scoffed and abruptly dropped my hand. "God, you're easy. I was only joking. Interesting, though, your reaction. I didn't think the mating bond would hit that strongly before you've even fucked him."

I grimaced in embarrassment, and Freyr snapped, "Could you have a little tact, please? Now, what do you want?"

"Just a couple things we need to discuss. It will only take a few minutes, then I'll have you back here with your whips and giant dildo before you can say—"

Freyr's foot connected with the middle of Stefan's stomach, sending the latter rocketing out the door and down the hall. He slid on his back for several feet and then jumped up, laughing hysterically.

After straightening his hair and clothes, Freyr put a finger under my chin and tipped my head up. "Sorry about him. He can be a bit uncouth." With a quick kiss, he said, "I'll come up as soon as I can. I love you."

"I love you too."

A shower would be nice, I decided, and I was relieved to find everything I needed without calling Lowner. Ten minutes under the scalding water felt amazing, but I wasn't sure if I should get dressed or not. Then I remembered I didn't have any clothes, so I got into bed naked. The cool, crisp sheets were like a million fingers, touching every nerve, but still I felt myself doze.

"I can feel you, pet," came that voice from Hell. *"Don't think that immortality will keep me from you. My brother will fall, and you will be mine."*

An image appeared, and I recoiled from the horror of Freyr's head rolling to a stop at my feet.

"No," I whispered in terror. "Freyr!"

"Shh. It was a dream, a bad dream." The voice was female and oddly familiar, but she was gone before I could open my eyes and ask her name. I was too exhausted to worry about it, and I nodded off again

I woke when I heard Freyr coming down the hall. When he opened the door, the delicious scent of him made my cock fill. The rustle of his clothes hitting the floor made me push aside all thoughts of the woman who had comforted me in my sleep.

"Are you awake?" Freyr asked quietly.

I decided to play with him a little, so I said nothing. He sighed and climbed under the covers, pulling me tight into his body. It was perfect. I surprised him by taking his hand and wrapping it around my rock-hard shaft. I chuckled and said, "Yes, I'm up."

The feel of Freyr's cool, smooth fingers gripping my dick was incredible, and the light kisses on the back of my neck threatened to undo me. He hummed against my ear. "You are so beautiful. Will you give yourself to me? Will you be my mate? Just because I feel it doesn't mean you must requite the affection. Perhaps we should wait until your memory improves."

"I want you. I feel it in the deepest parts of me—you are my mate. Please." I turned in his hold and took his index finger and sucked it into my mouth. He hissed in pleasure while I worked it with my tongue as if it was his cock. Then I put my leg up over his hip and said, "Take me."

"Fuck," he croaked, and rolled onto his back. I straddled his hips and leaned forward to kiss him. I was rewarded when his wet finger tickled my hole.

"Oh my God, yes," I moaned. "Touch me."

"You're so perfect." A tip of his finger pushed inside me.

"Don't tease me. I want more."

"Just wait."

"No."

"Lube."

"Right."

He laughed and I heard a drawer open and close. The soft click of the bottle cap was followed by a cool, wet finger slipping into me.

"More."

"I have to be gentle. It's been a long time for you."

"*More!*" I whined. "It doesn't hurt. I need it!"

Very quickly, a second finger joined the first, and he pounded his hand against my ass. When he started to tease my prostate, I bucked. "Holy shit. I'm not going to last if you don't stop that."

"I won't last long either. I'm sorry this won't be gentle, but—"

"Just. Fuck. Me." I demanded.

He slicked his cock, and with a quiet, "I love you," he pushed up into me. Burning pain gave way to unbelievable pleasure as I lowered myself onto that thick, long cock. We both moaned and whimpered with the sheer pleasure of it.

His fangs scratched my shoulder. "I need your blood now, Carter. Give yourself to me."

Instinctively, I turned my head, exposing my pulsing artery to him. "I'm yours. Take me, and show me how good it can be."

He looked deep into my eyes, as if searching for any remaining trace of doubt. Finding none, he brought his mouth to my throat and bit. A thousand sensations raced through me—the stab of his bite, the pull of his suckling, his wet, hot tongue twisting and turning, seeking my blood.

Freyr's cock slammed into me so deeply my ring stretched on every stroke. His fingers dug into my hips, and I winced when he pulled too hard, but I ignored the pain, focusing on the way he fucked me. It was primal, hard sex. Nothing else could have satisfied our need for each other at that moment.

Just before he came, he tipped his head back and roared loudly, like an animal staking its claim. Blood colored his lips and dripped down his chin. "Mine. You're finally mine!" he cried, and his cock pulsed inside me. He returned to feed again, and his hand wrapped around my hard cock.

"Yes. Oh, fuck." With efficient skill, he twisted and stroked, and I came all over his stomach.

He took his mouth off my neck and licked the wound closed. Then he fell back against the pillows. "How do you feel?"

"I feel like I'm yours. Did I taste good?"

"There isn't a strong enough word for how your blood tastes. I'm spoiled to any blood but yours now."

"That's a good thing." My hand traveled down my stomach, and over my omnipresent erection.

Freyr took my mouth in a kiss so hard he knocked our fangs together. We both grunted, but didn't care. He asked, "Can I have you again?"

"Fuck, yes," I replied. I flipped onto my stomach, straight as a plank and said, "Cover me. I really want to feel it."

He lay atop me and said, "Carter, you have the most delectable ass."

"It's all yours."

"Mm. Mine." He thrust into me and drove me into the mattress. Arms outstretched and fingers intertwined, we fucked for what seemed like hours until a loud moan betokened Freyr's orgasm. I wasn't far behind.

I sighed. "I love you so much."

Freyr rolled onto his side, and pulled out gently. "Feeling's mutual." He stood and pulled on his pants. I sat up. "Where are you going?"

He smiled ruefully. "I have a conference call with a security firm in London, and it's now morning there. I'll be as quick as possible, okay?"

I wasn't thrilled about it, but I didn't want to appear too clingy. I kissed him and rolled over. Sleep came quickly.

Another nightmare haunted my sleep, but my angel chased it away, sending a comforting chill through my body. Heat flowed through me and I opened my eyes.

I saw no one, but I heard a woman whisper, "Hello, Carter."

She sounded like the same woman as before. I asked, "Who are you?"

A pale hand covered my own, but the woman who owned it was still in shadow. I tried to focus on her, but in my half-conscious state, all I could see was a blur of a face crowned with long blonde hair.

She let go of my hand and backed farther into the dark corner. "You know who I am."

I was certain I'd known her. I recognized the voice. "Where have you been?"

She hesitated. "I've been away."

"Away where?"

"Shh. No one must know that I've seen you, so don't tell them. Just be ready. I'll come for you soon, and we can go away together. We can get away from them."

"Why can't I tell them?"

"Because I know the secret," she whispered.

"What secret?"

For the first time, she leaned into my field of vision. I was so dizzy, however, that I couldn't bring her features into focus. All I could make out was long, blond hair and blue eyes. She flicked her gaze toward the door, then breathed, "Alder didn't kill our parents. Freyr did."

"*Our* parents?" I breathed. "Lidell? Please, come here."

"They mustn't find me. Goodbye, Carter." She went to the window and dropped out of sight. In my stupor, I followed her, falling clumsily to the ground with a thud. I shook my head to try and clear the fuzz, and saw her darting through a thin patch of birch saplings. A ghostly laugh floated back to me. I called to her, but my knees wouldn't support me anymore. I lay on the damp grass and sobbed.

"Carter!" Stefan called. "Frey, he's here. Carter, what the hell did you do?"

I growled and twisted from his grip. "Get away from me."

He put his hands up and took a step back. "What the fuck?"

Freyr arrived then. He looked at Stefan, then at me. "Carter? What are you doing out here?"

"Get back!" I yelled.

"What?"

"You lied to me. You killed my parents."

Freyr's voice was anguished. "How could you think that? Of course I didn't kill your parents. I love you. You're confused, my love. Come in and—" He reached a hand out to me and I snapped at it. His patience evaporated. "This is insane. You are coming inside with me."

"No!" I yelled, backing away from the house.

"*Herr Amsel!*" someone called from the window of my room. The young vampire jumped down and raced over to us, holding something in his hand. "*Herr Amsel. Ich habe eine Spritze gefunden.*"

He handed the find to Freyr and I gasped—it was a syringe, half-full of blood.

"That explains the paranoia," Stefan said. "But who could it have been?"

I smiled slightly. "I know exactly who it was."

Everyone turned to me, and Freyr said, "Tell me, Carter."

"It was my sister, Lidell."

They all looked around nervously. Freyr said, "Look. Let's go back inside and talk about this. Now."

Reluctantly, I followed him into the great room. Stefan turned to me.

"It couldn't have been Lidell in your room. There may have been a woman, but it wasn't your sister. That was a hallucination."

"It was *her*!" I roared. My body seethed with rage, and everyone, including Freyr, backed away slowly. Fire burned in my eyes, and a white-hot anger boiled in my blood. My fangs lengthened and poked into my lip. My pulse rushed in my ears. Finally, I closed my eyes and concentrated on calming down. The heat dulled, and I exhaled slowly.

When I looked up, Freyr was studying me with incredulity. "Are you feeling all right, my love?"

"I am now," I replied. "Kinda light-headed. Sorry if I snapped at you."

"*Snapped?*" Stefan repeated. "That's one way to put it."

A short snarl passed my lips, and I gritted my teeth. "Pardon me, but I'm tired, and I don't think it was just a dream."

The young man who'd recovered the syringe cleared his throat nervously. "Excuse me, sir, but IVAS is very powerful."

"What's IVAS?" I sat cross-legged on an over-stuffed sofa, scowling at Stefan as he paced up and down the room, deep in thought.

"Intravenous administered self-feed," Stefan explained, then stopped and turned a sad gaze on me. "Lidell is dead, Carter. I buried her myself. Her, your mother, your father—I buried them all. Alder is behind this. He must have found someone who looks like your sister."

"It was her," I repeated obstinately.

Nerves frazzled, Stefan threw up his hands and yelled, "No, it wasn't!" The lampshades rattled.

"Enough," Freyr said. "Whatever happened, we know that

someone was in Carter's room tonight. What *I* want to know is where the fucking guards were!" He raged around the room. "Do any of you understand what could have happened?"

Stefan stepped in his path. "Frey, we were still trying to set up posts. You came home a day early."

"That's no excuse. Get rid of them. They all die." The condemned groaned and whimpered, but Stefan wasn't about to kill his own men. He stared at Freyr as though he'd gone insane, but made no move to follow the absurd order.

"Have you lost your mind?" he asked in shock.

"Do as I say!" Freyr barked.

With a mock salute, Stefan said, *"Heil Herr von Drubich!"*

Freyr shoved him backward. "Don't you dare call me that."

Stefan shoved Freyr just as hard. "That's how you're acting. Kill them? You *have* gone mad. Have you forgotten who the enemy is, *Secundus?*" he sneered. Pointing toward the guards, he barked, "Is it them? Is it me? I know that your mate means everything to you, but you cannot forget your pledge to them — that you would never become the tyrant your brother is. If this is how you'll treat those who have stood by you for centuries, I won't be part of it."

Freyr's eyes widened and his mouth opened and closed. He bowed his head, and turned away. "I . . . I'm sorry," he said in a small, weary voice. "You're right, Stefan. Once again, you're the wise one."

The giant vampire put a hand on Freyr's shoulder. "It's forgiven, but we can't fight Alder if we're all fighting each other."

"Yes," my mate said. "We'll face this evil together. As for the guard . . ." All of the men stiffened. "I apologize for losing my temper. You may go, with my thanks, but please make sure that posts are filled immediately."

All twelve men glanced at each other for a few seconds before scrambling through every available exit, including windows. I wanted to laugh at them, but the events of the night had truly disturbed me. I just wanted to be alone with Freyr.

Stefan stood in the doorway, frowning. "We should talk, Frey."

"Yes. I believe we must."

He took a step toward the door, but I grabbed his hand. "Please. I just want to get some sleep with you. I'm . . . scared. Come to bed."

With a fatherly kiss to my forehead, he said, "You're safe, Carter. The guards are outside, and there will be two men at the door."

"But—"

"I'm sorry. I wouldn't go if it wasn't important. We have to figure this out. I'll be back shortly." He and Stefan walked toward the office, leaving me with my retinue of bodyguards.

I was so pissed I could barely breathe. Every two seconds he was leaving me to go chat with Stefan about something. Couldn't he spend a little time with me?

I went up to our bedroom and fell down on the bed. I punched the pillow, forgetting my strength, and broke a coil in the mattress. "Shit! It figures. Well, he can sleep on that side."

Chapter Six—Freyr

Stefan handed me a glass.

"What's this?" I eyed the amber contents suspiciously.

"Piss." Stefan laughed. "What do you think? McGillun found the recipe for *Apfelwein*."

"You're joking!"

Apple wine had been a staple of our clan during the nineteenth century. Vampires could eat as much human food as they wished, and it did curb our appetite for very short periods of time. The problem was it all tasted like shit. Stefan and I had first tried apple wine during a trip to Frankfort in the early 1800s. It was a local specialty—a slightly sweet cider with a low alcohol content, which was easier for us to digest than straight ale. The taste wasn't nearly as bad as beers that most taverns served, either, so we drank that when we had to appear to blend in with the human population. One sure way to be noticed as outsiders was to spend any time with Germans and not drink anything.

After returning home from that trip, we tried making the wine ourselves. Nearly everyone in the clan liked it, although Lowner threatened more than once to smash every bottle if we didn't stop spilling it on the furniture. Eventually, we ran out, and our lives got too hectic to keep up with such a meaningless fancy. After Berlin, when the clans split, the recipe was lost and the wine forgotten.

Now here it was again, the same rich golden brown I remembered. I held my glass up in salute and said, "*Prost*." Stefan did the same.

After one sip, we both grimaced. Stefan set the glass down and said, "Evidently, McGillun needs more practice."

"Either that or we've lost the taste for it."

"We'll have to drink it, though. She's made six bottles."

My stomach turned and I remembered the real reason for our visit. "What are we going to do, Stefan?"

"Well, I had the blood in the syringe tested. Let me called Samad and see if he's found anything."

Samad was the resident genius-inventor-hacker who had joined the clan only a few months before Carter woke up. He was then working on a new DNA extractor that would—he hoped—be able to break down and identify vampire blood in minutes, rather than days. Since our blood didn't have the contaminants human blood carried, it was a much quicker process.

Stefan dialed his number. "How's the new gadget coming? So it worked? It gave you results already? Hang on, you lost me. If not his, then whose was it?" Upon hearing the answer, he ended the call, sank into a chair and rubbed his hands over his face.

"What's wrong?" I asked cautiously.

"You won't like the results. It wasn't all Carter's blood."

My eyes bulged. "What? Whose was it?"

"We aren't certain, but there was a partial DNA match."

"Who, God damn it? Tell me! Whose DNA?"

Stefan sat back and looked me straight in the eye. "Yours."

I was stupefied. "Mine? I didn't put my blood in that syringe! Are you crazy?"

"Frey, I said it was a *partial* match. It was a close blood relative of yours."

"Oh my God . . . Alder!"

He nodded. "Whoever was in Carter's room must have brought a mixture of Alder's and Carter's blood with them."

"That's crazy. How would they have had access to Carter's

blood?"

"I can't figure that out yet," he admitted.

I put my head in my hands and tried to think of where it could have come from. When the answer struck me, I almost laughed. "The clinic. Carter's IVAS supply was in the cooler with all of the other patients' medications. Any one of the staff would have had access."

Stefan closed his eyes and groaned. "Oh Christ. I'll go to the clinic and find out if anything strange has been going on. We'll check the employment files, and Levi will go through the video feeds."

He stood up and pulled out his phone. As he typed, he said, "We'll start with the day Jacob died. Everyone knew we were bringing Carter out of his coma. I'd imagine they started to plan everything then. It's perfect. They must have known we wouldn't be using any more of Carter's IVAS, so no one would notice if some of it was missing."

"And I told him I'd protect him," I said miserably. "What will this do to him? You saw his explosion just now. Do you think he'll become like my brother? And what does that mean as far as mating goes? They've exchanged blood sources, it's going to—"

Stefan put a hand on my shoulder to stop my ranting. "Frey, we'll deal with this. You've waited so patiently, without complaint, for ten months. You deserve to be happy. Carter is completely devoted to you, so why don't you get out of here and go show him how you feel?"

My mate was in a deep sleep when I got back to the room—most likely a side effect of the IVAS. I sighed with disappointment and went to the window. When I opened it and stuck my head out, the four guards on the ground below the window immediately turned up to look at me. Reassured by how alert the guard was, I went to the bed and pulled back the blankets. Carter wore loose-fitting sleep pants and no shirt. The way he was curled up, with his ass thrust backward, accentuated the two dimples at the bottom of his spine. My fangs lengthened, and my cheeks hurt with want.

"The hell with this." I stripped quickly and climbed in behind my mate.

When I put a hand on his hip and kissed his neck, he stirred and mumbled in his sleep. "Mm. I want you."

My already-stiff cock became hard as steel and I scooted down further. "You are so perfect," I whispered against the soft skin at the small of his back. "So brave, so beautiful, so precious to me. Give me your blood, Carter."

One mate's heart can call to its partner in amazing ways. My need was answered by Carter's heart. Without fully waking, he pushed his pants down and kicked them off. Then he lay on his back, lifted his knees and pointed to where the femoral artery ran closest to his groin.

I made a strange choking sound before I could say, "Oh, gods preserve me." Kneeling in front of him, I put my hands on his ass and spread him wide. The wrinkled opening pulsed, and I leaned down to claim my prize.

Carter moaned when I slowly dragged the flat of my tongue from the tip of his tailbone over his hole and up to burrow in his sac.

His eyes opened to narrow slits, and he smiled. "For fuck's sake, do that again."

"My pleasure, love." I keep the pressure heavy until I got to his pucker again, and I feathered the tip of my tongue over it. When he began to whimper and tremble, I went farther and nuzzled my nose against his balls. The heady scent drew the venom to my tongue, and I prepared to bite.

I retrieved lube from the nightstand, slicked my fingers, and slowly sank them into Carter's ass. I massaged his prostate lightly, and he thrashed under me. I could no longer withstand the temptation. While pumping my fingers hard in and out of Carter's ass, I wrapped an arm around his right thigh and bit the spot where it met his groin.

Carter opened his eyes wide and gasped. "Oh, fuck yes!" he cried.

His long fingers twisted in my hair, holding me to his leg. The sweet, sticky flow coated my tongue, and I felt my orgasm already building. I was amazed that taking my mate's blood was enough to make me come, even though I hadn't touched myself. A string of pre-come stretched from the tip of my cock to the mattress.

All too quickly, I felt the subtle shift in Carter's blood pressure and knew I couldn't take any more. He thrashed and moaned as I twisted and turned my tongue languidly over the puncture. The reaction was more than I could take, and I emptied my balls onto the sheet. Again and again my cock pulsed, releasing my pleasure in gradually decreasing waves.

"Carter," I sighed. "I love you, my mate."

His breaths became shorter and shorter. I took his entire cock in my mouth, then pulled back very slowly while I thrust my fingers over and over against his prostate.

"Fuck!" he roared, and dug his nails into my scalp. His back arched off the bed, and his body went stiff as a board. I'd never seen anyone come as powerfully as my mate did at that moment. His cock exploded, and I couldn't keep up with the amount of cum that shot into my mouth and down my throat. It dribbled down my chin and into the dark hair covering Carter's balls.

He shivered and shook with the effort of his orgasm, so I drew the blankets over us.

"That was incredible to witness," I said, kissing his throat tenderly.

"Ha! It was more incredible to feel. It felt like you fucking tasered my prostate."

We both exploded in laughter, but he quickly lost steam and fell asleep. I spent some time just looking at his face, admiring the way the moonlight made his skin appear a ghostly gray. I was so afraid for him that my heart ached. In the morning, I would have to tell him that Alder's blood—however miniscule the amount—now ran through his veins.

CHAPTER EIGHT—CARTER

Freyr was still sleeping when I got up to shower. After the stress of the night before, I thought I'd let him have a late morning while I explored the house. I opened the bedroom door and gasped. Two tall, very muscular vampires turned from their sentry posts to face me. The realization they'd been there all night, and had therefore heard Freyr and me in bed together, embarrassed me to no end.

One of the behemoths blinked at me with no expression. The other smiled nervously, and said, "*Guten morgen, mein Herr.*"

I smiled and said, "Excuse me. Gotta head down and see what's going on." The men glanced at each other, then back at me with confused looks. I summoned as much college German as I could and mumbled, "Damn, I can't remember how to say it. I go to dee kookuh?"

The guard who had bid me good morning smiled. "*Ja, komm mit.*"

He gave his mute companion instructions and led me downstairs to a cavernous kitchen. To the right of the door was a butcher-block island that separated the sink, stove, and refrigerator from a large farm table, whose paint had long been rubbed away by plates and elbows. A dozen mismatched chairs surrounded it, all taken by other vampires. The room was a bustling hive, apparently the command center for the day's activities.

Lowner stood in the garden door, shouting at someone I couldn't see. "No, dahlias, not lilies! No, those are tulips. In

the greenhouse. The green—Oh, forget it. I'll do it myself."
When he turned and saw me, he smiled broadly. "Good
morning, Mr. Denwright. Would you like to have some breakfast?"

"Huh?" I asked in confusion. I looked around at everyone
in the room, trying to figure out which vampire would let me
feed from him.

Lowner saw my reaction and chuckled. "No, sir. I was
thinking of *real* food—porridge or fruit or something."

I felt like a complete imbecile. Alder had never eaten—
while I was around anyway—so I figured vampires just drank
blood. One of the guards offered me a chair at the head of the
table and I sank into it. "I didn't know we could—"

"Yes, thank the gods," a tall, dark-haired vampire said, as
he bit into an apple.

"Oh," I muttered.

The man extended his hand and introduced himself. "I'm
Kirner, Captain of the Guard."

"Nice to meet you."

He nodded and continued in a thick, German accent. "Yes,
the new vampires are more okay with food. It tastes still very
good. If you are ancient as Herr Amsel or as Stefan, your
tongue does not it like, but still you can do it."

"Watch it, Kirner," Stefan said, trying not to laugh.

"It's the same as the sun. It doesn't do a thing to us." The
speaker was a beautiful young woman of about twenty, with
short, spiky, blonde hair, and the most startling eyes I'd ever
seen. They were the same hue as the inside of a ruby grape-
fruit, like pink sapphires, deep and crystalline. I had never
beheld anything so mesmerizing, and I leaned farther over the
corner of the table to get a closer look. She leaned toward me
until her forehead rested on mine, then said, "Oh my God.
Can you read minds?"

"Stop that," Lowner snapped.

The pixie sat back and winked. "I'm Greta, by the way. And yeah, my eyes are pink. Kinda cool, huh?"

I nodded. "They're beautiful. Um . . . Lowner, I think I'll try to eat something."

His eyes sparkled, and he rubbed his hands together excitedly. "Excellent. What would you like? Pancakes, waffles, omelet?"

My stomach grumbled at the delicious offerings, but there was one thing I suddenly craved. I asked, "You wouldn't happen to have blueberry muffins? They are — *were,* my favorite."

Lowner clucked his tongue. "I'm afraid I don't have any blueberries, but I'll get them for tomorrow."

Stefan curled his lip. "Mm. Blueberries. Little, indigo globes of goo."

"Stefan," Lowner scolded. "That's quite rude. They are for Mr. Denwright."

My creator shook his head at me. "Sometimes I wonder if this boy is really mine."

We all laughed and he picked up the newspaper. I decided on pancakes, and was served an enormous stack, swimming in fresh butter. Lowner's assistant housekeeper, McGillun, fetched a pitcher of maple syrup from the butler's pantry, and I dumped it on with a giddy grin. As apprehensive as I was about how human food would taste, I was delighted with the reality — sweet and fluffy with a hint of tangy buttermilk. I gulped down six before I realized what I'd done.

I stared in horror at the empty plate. "I can't believe I ate so much."

Lowner's eyes shone with pride. "Would you like more?"

"Thanks, but no. Stefan, can I do the crossword?"

"Certainly," he said. "Greta only got one answer."

She stuck her tongue out at him and handed me a pencil. I began the puzzle, but soon realized it was a futile effort. I slammed it down and said, "God damn it! All of these friggin' clues have to do with recent events and movies and I can't remember . . . shit. I feel like Rip van Winkle."

"At least you're still young and hot," Greta teased. "We'll just have to get you a tutor."

When a dark-haired man in his early twenties entered the room, everyone else stopped talking and glanced at each other, smirking. Stefan cleared his throat and concentrated on the sports section, studiously ignoring the newcomer.

The young vamp was as gorgeous as the rest, but more exotic—dark bronzed skin and black hair that glimmered with blue. Eyes the color of butterscotch flicked quickly toward Stefan before coming to rest on my face. He spoke with a thick accent. "Hello, sir. I'm honored to meet you. My name is Samad El-Effendi. I'm sort of new here too."

He seemed really nervous, so I tried to keep up the conversation. "Please, call me Carter. How long have you been here?"

"About four months. Mr. Gebhart"—he pointed to Stefan—"came to Egypt to bring me here after some of the Watch found me wandering the streets of Luxor. I had awoken as a vampire with no memory of what had happened to me."

"What's the Watch?" I asked.

Stefan lowered the paper. "There are vampires all over the world who keep track of newborns to prevent any . . . unfortunate occurrences. When they find changelings with no clan or resources to turn to, my team and I collect them and bring them here."

"Are there a lot of newborns?" I asked. "Other vampires just go around creating others?"

"Some do," Kirner said. "Most often those come from Alder's groups."

The name gave me the shivers, and Greta patted my back. "That's enough, Kirner."

He looked miserably rueful. "I did not think, Mr. Denwright. I apologize."

I tried to smile. "It's fine. Just saying his name's not going to hurt me. And call me Carter, *please,* all of you."

Lowner announced a fresh pot of coffee, and Samad asked for a cup. When he reached across the table, his arm passed close by Stefan's face. The latter inhaled suddenly, and Samad fell back in his seat, sipping his coffee in silence.

Stefan rose abruptly. "I have some business to attend to. Kirner, I want you to set up patrol for this morning. I'll be in my office, not to be disturbed."

When we heard Stefan's boots clunk up the stairs, Samad let his head fall onto the wooden table with a thud. "Oh my God," he groaned.

Greta rested her cheek on his shoulder. "Don't worry, Sam. He'll figure it out."

Since no one was offering any information, I asked, "Am I missing something here?"

Greta said, "Ever since Sam came to live with us, Stefan's been a raging asshole, and we all know why."

"Why?" I asked.

Lowner slapped a dishrag on the counter. "Because Stefan is hopelessly attracted to our child of the pharaohs here, but he's too stupid to admit it."

"Attracted," I repeated. "As in . . ."

Lowner nodded. "As in Stefan's found his mate, but for some reason he doesn't feel he deserves him. The man acts like a befrigged martyr."

"That sucks," I said. "Sorry, Samad. Maybe he'll figure it out soon. Just be patient."

He shrugged and bit into a piece of toast. My heart hurt for him, and I wished there was something I could do to help.

After breakfast, I went to find my own mate, already

plotting how to get Stefan to claim his man. I found him in the office and told him what I'd learned at the breakfast table.

He scowled at me. "Don't you dare."

"Don't I dare what?" I asked indignantly.

Freyr put his pen down and looked severely at me. "You don't know Stefan. He will be royally pissed if he finds out what you're up to."

"I'm not up to anything," I said. "I'm just helping things along."

He shook his head and went back to his paperwork, so I decided to capture his attention in a less direct way. Crawling past his knees, I got into the space under his desk. The carved oak panel in front would hide me from anyone who came in.

"What are you doing?" he asked.

"Serving my mate," I whispered. "Scoot toward the edge of the chair."

An evil grin darkened his face and he pulled his chair close to the desk, locking me in. "Now serve," he commanded.

I ran my hand over the bulge straining his zipper and freed it from its prison. It sprang out at me with a drip of pre-cum just peeking out from the slit. Each time I saw Freyr's cock, it was like my birthday. That powerful, pleasurable tool was all mine, to use any way I liked. I licked the tip and sighed. The exquisite taste of salty, sweet musk made my own dick press painfully against my jeans. I slid down as far as I could in such a cramped position, wrapped my lips around him, and covered the last remaining inches with my fingers. I hummed and twisted my hands like corkscrews, and even more pre-cum slicked the tip.

As I sucked him deep into my mouth, there was a knock at the door. I panicked and tried to pull off Freyr's dick, but he held me there with a strong hand to the back of my head.

"Yes?"

The door opened, and I heard Lowner's voice. "Good

morning, sir. Do you know where Mr. Denwright is?"

I tried again to move, but Freyr had me trapped, so I worked my finger into his pants and pushed the tip against his tight hole.

"Ah!" he yelped.

"Are you all right, sir?" Lowner asked.

"Fine," he replied in a squeak. "Ahem, fine. No, I don't know where he is, and I have a lot of work to do, so tell everyone I am not to be disturbed."

"Yes, sir."

The door closed again. Freyr pulled me out from under the desk and hauled me to my feet. "You'll pay for that," he said against my neck. With a light nip, he asked, "Up for something a little daring?"

I didn't believe him. It was a highly visible, public location. "Here?"

"Yes," was the growled reply. "Let's inaugurate my desk, shall we?"

"Are you going to lock the door?" I asked.

He did as I asked. His cock bobbed lewdly as he walked. I licked my lips, wishing I'd been able to finish him with my mouth. As much as I wanted him to fuck me, I also loved the flavor of his seed, and wanted it constantly.

"God, you're gorgeous," I said. The sight of my mate, pants halfway down his thighs, cock hard and dripping, was enough to make me blow my load, but when he loosened his tie and slid it from his collar.

I smiled and said, "Are you going to tie me up?"

"You want that?" he asked with concern. "I mean, it may not be such a good idea, Carter."

"Please take me," I whimpered. Licking my lips, I rubbed my body against his. "Let's play."

Freyr took the bait. "Bend over the desk with your hands behind your back."

I chuckled and turned around. The silk was cool against my skin as he pulled it tight around my wrists. I'd never done bondage with a lover before. Of course, Alder had bound me, but that had nothing to do with the *real* idea of bondage — that was about torture. Freyr was exploring my boundaries, testing my limits. Alder crushed my boundaries and broke my spirit.

Freyr's smooth fingers caressed my ass cheeks. I sighed, anticipating the head of a slick cock, or perhaps a wet tongue. What I received, however, was a hard, flat hand, brought down on my butt with a reverberating smack.

I cried out in pain and tried to wiggle from his grip. Another smack burned my skin like an iron. Inexplicably, the pain went straight to my cock, as it rubbed uncomfortably against the blotter on the desk. I hissed at the friction.

Freyr stopped the spanking and stood back. "I hurt you. We should stop."

"Please don't stop," I moaned. "I like it. Please, Freyr."

He kissed the back of my neck and nipped my ear with his fangs. Then he spit on his fingers. "Sorry. No lube."

"God, I don't care. Just fuck me."

"Holy shit," he breathed. Holding my bound wrists in one hand and my hip in the other, Freyr entered me in one long push. As much as I had wanted to be taken like this, I was suddenly transported back to the horrible days before I became a vampire. I panicked.

"Let me go, Freyr," I said. "I don't like this."

He thought I was playing the part. "Be quiet," he hissed and thrust hard against my hips. Another smack, then another and tears streamed from my eyes. As he fucked me, horrible dreams and fears flooded my mind, and I broke. I was once again in the small, dark room, bleeding and tortured.

I sobbed, "No, Alder! Please don't hurt me anymore."

Freyr gasped and untied my hands. I collapsed on the desk,

sobbing, and he fled to the far corner of the room. "I'm sorry, Carter. My God, please forgive me."

Stefan had heard my scream and burst through the locked door. Greta and Sam followed, mouths agape at the strange scene before them. I hurried to pull up my pants. Stefan looked to Freyr. "What the hell's going on?" he demanded.

Freyr could barely speak. "I ... didn't think. We were just ... and I got rough with him."

"You fool!" Stefan roared. "Don't you remember what Alder did to him?"

"It was my fault," I said quickly, trying to defuse Stefan's wrath. "I ... asked him to."

"No," Freyr insisted. "I should never have done that. Carter, I'm so sorry. I would never hurt you."

I took a step toward my mate, but he put his hands up and backed away. I sighed. "Freyr, please talk to me. I'm sorry I reacted that way. I guess I should've had a safeword or something. Or maybe I wasn't ready to do that, but I'm fine, honey."

Freyr shook his head. "I hurt you. I can't forgive myself for that." I reached for him again, but he jumped out a window and disappeared across the lawn.

"Let him go," Stefan said. "He'll be back eventually."

Freyr didn't come to bed that night, or the next. His cell phone was off, and I left at least twenty messages and texts. After four days without a word, the entire household was tense and on edge. Sam and Greta had become good friends to me, and they worked hard to make me believe everything was fine. On the fourth day, I stuck my head into Stefan's office, hoping for news. He looked at me with pity and shook his head. I could tell he was getting worried too.

That evening, I had to feed on one of the staff, because I'd used up my energy worrying and waiting for Freyr to come home. Quincy, one of the commanders of the guard, volunteered to be my donor. I had my meal in the kitchen, in front of a half-dozen other vampires, to avoid any awkwardness of being alone with Quincy, and it worked. Biting his wrist with a group of people watching kept every sexual nerve completely anesthetized. If anything, my dick went into hiding.

I thanked him, and he went to Lowner. The older man kissed my donor's temple, and I saw Lowner's hand grip Quincy's ass. Their mouths met and their tongues danced, and I wanted Freyr more than ever. I missed my mate.

"Excuse me," I muttered, and went to my room. I shuffled up the stairs, dreading the empty bed that awaited me. Part of me wondered if Freyr would ever return, and if he didn't, how I was supposed to go on without my mate.

Opening the door with a lazy push, I scratched my head and yawned. Something by the window moved, and I turned quickly to see a wet, muddy, miserable Freyr standing in the corner. I gasped and put a hand on the wall to steady myself.

"Miss me?" he asked.

My temper exploded. "You're kidding, right? You take off for days without any of us knowing where you were and you're asking if I *missed* you? I want to fucking *kill* you!"

"Carter, I—"

"Carter, I, nothing," I snapped. "I know that everything last week got fucked up, and I know that you weren't really trying to hurt me, but the least you could have done was to stick around and talk to me about it, instead of running away. J*esus!* Where the fuck were you?"

"Canada," he said calmly. "The Yukon, I think."

"The Yukon—what? Why?"

"Because I had to think."

I growled in frustration. "You had to think? About what?" He reached out for me, but I wrinkled my nose. "You're filthy and smell like elk. Take a shower."

He walked past me and grinned. His smile always got to me, so I melted a little and followed him into our bathroom. As he shucked off his clothes, I studied his muscular form and bit my lip to keep my arousal at bay.

"So," I began, "what were you thinking about for four days?"

He stepped into the hot water and let out a long, exhausted sigh. "About how to tell you something."

"Hang on a minute. You left so you could figure out how to tell me something? Usually staying within a few thousand miles of someone is a more effective way of communicating."

"I know, love. I'm sorry. Will you join me?"

"No."

A long, dripping-wet arm reached around the frosted-glass shower enclosure and the hand waved me over.

"No," I repeated firmly.

The hand clenched into a fist, then just the middle finger raised. I laughed until the finger wiggled as though he was going for my prostate. I started undressing as quickly as possible.

"Not fair," I growled, stepping into the shower with Freyr. He put a hand around my waist and pulled me against his warm, wet body. I shivered and reached up to kiss him. "I'm still mad at you."

"I know," he muttered.

I poured my coconut and mango scented shower gel on my hands and began massaging his shoulders. "Well? Are you going to tell me what's so important?"

After a moment, he said, "When you were given that syringe of blood last week, it wasn't just your blood in it."

I swallowed hard, dreading the answer to my next question. I choked on my words. "Wh-Whose blood was it?"

Freyr turned to look me in the eye. "It was Alder's. He apparently stole some of your IVAS supply at the clinic."

"Alder." I felt sick to my core, and the blood I'd just drank threatened to reemerge. Worse than that sensation, however, was the echo of a terrifyingly familiar laugh in my head. I staggered back against the cool tiled wall and Freyr hurried to catch me.

"Carter, look at me."

I shook my head violently and shied away from him. The implications of the news were clear immediately. If I had Alder's blood in my body, did that mean I was mated to him?

"No, no, no," I murmured.

Freyr cupped my cheek with his hand and forced me to look at him. "I know what you're thinking," he said, "but it's not true. Just because some of Alder's blood flows through you doesn't mean he's your mate."

"But—"

"*I* am your mate, Carter. It's *my* blood that calms your thirst, *my* blood that makes your heart race. You own me. Every part of me is devoted to you, for eternity. Now, drink."

He tilted his head to the side, and I bit without hesitation.

CHAPTER NINE—CARTER

Several weeks went by without further effects from the tainted blood. I came to the conclusion Alder had used it only to confuse Freyr, and to scare the crap out of me. At any rate, I was profoundly relieved I wasn't going to turn into a raving psychopath. All those around me were glad, too. Members of the guard were still going through security footage from the clinic, but it was a slow process. Since we were dealing with vampires who could move with lightning speed, the footage had to be watched nearly in real time to avoid missing anything. Until they found some clue as to my night visitor's identity, all we could do was wait.

In early August, Greta came bouncing into the kitchen during breakfast and called, "Freyr! Freyr!"

"Yes, yes!" he replied with mock enthusiasm.

She rolled her eyes but didn't let him derail her excitement. "I got a call from the breeder, and the puppies are ready. I can go up today and pick out—"

He put up a hand to stop her. "Hold on. I didn't say yes, Greta. I said I'd think about a dog. That doesn't mean yes. I really don't think it's a good idea."

Her pink eyes widened, and her bottom lip quivered. It was extremely effective, and I only wished I could pull it off like she did. She balled up her fists and stomped her foot. "You never let me have anything I want!"

"Except a sports car," Quincy said.

Greta punched him on the arm. "Shut up, Quincy! That's different. I *have* to drive."

"Yes," Freyr said, "but you don't *need* a dog."

Loath as I was to admit it, I didn't know vampires could have dogs. The old Hollywood plot of "vampires scare every other animal away," came to mind. Apparently I was wrong.

Greta resorted to a high-pitched whine. "I want a dog!" she cried, then began yanking on Freyr's suit. He batted her away.

She sat down next to Sam, crossed her arms and huffed. At first, I thought she was going to give up, but then I saw her reach over and pinch Sam's arm.

He winced and stuttered, "I th-think having a dog would be fun." He flicked his eyes at Stefan, who looked back at him over the top of the paper.

I had to smile. They'd been exchanging glances like that more and more frequently, and even played cribbage or watched movies together some evenings. Goosebumps tingled on my skin when I thought they might soon tell each other how they felt.

After a minute, Stefan said, "We could train a dog as protection, Frey."

Sam and Greta exchanged conspiratorial smiles.

Freyr glared at Stefan. "Whose fucking side are you on?"

"What harm would it do?" he replied.

Lowner growled. "I'll tell you what harm! Chewed furniture, urine stains everywhere, and the smell—God help us— *the smell* of wet dog." He pretended to choke himself.

"I'll clean up after it, I promise!" Greta pleaded.

Freyr raised an eyebrow. "Just like they promised the Hindenburg was safe."

Sam looked like a puppy himself, his mournful eyes staring at me, as though they were saying, *"Please, help us. Please, Carter."* I slid closer to Freyr and leaned my cheek against his arm. Normally, he loved when I did that, but he wasn't buying. He put his index finger on my forehead and pushed me back into my chair.

"Don't even try the pouty thing. You've never been able to pout convincingly."

I narrowed my eyes and tried a different avenue of attack. While carrying on a conversation with Sam and Greta about the latest teenage vampire drama on television, I curled my hand around Freyr's thigh and kneaded it hard. I was impressed when he didn't moan or grunt or even flinch. But I was on a mission, so I brought my hand up his leg slowly until I brushed against his cock. It twitched under my fingers, and I knew I had him.

"Come on, Freyr. I'd like to have a dog." I emphasized my point by squeezing him and tracing my fingers over his balls.

A little cough escaped him, and he inhaled sharply. "Don't I get a say in what happens in my own house?"

"No," Greta and I both said.

He rolled up the paper and tapped it against the table. We all stared at him, waiting for his verdict. Finally, he said, "Fine."

"Thank you, thank you, thank you!" Greta chirped.

"But —" Freyr said with an evil grin. "Stefan will be responsible for making sure it's taken care of."

Stefan didn't answer. He was staring at Sam. Sam was trying to look anywhere but into Stefan's eyes, but he wasn't succeeding. I was surprised how openly they were flirting. Freyr repeated his statement, but Stefan still didn't hear him. I cleared my throat to get his attention, and Stefan murmured, "Mm?" without looking away from the man we all knew he loved.

"Stefan!" Freyr barked.

Stefan jumped and turned. "Um . . . sorry, what?"

"For Christ's sake!" my mate groaned. "Just make sure they all take care of the damn dog."

"Why me?"

Freyr chuckled. "Because you're the one who sponsored

the bill. Now you have to stand behind it. I'll see you all later. I have to go into the city for a while." He bent down to kiss me and left before I could grab his tie and yank him down for another.

Greta hopped up and pulled Sam with her. "Come on. We have to go to the breeders."

Sam asked her to wait a minute. "Excuse me, Stefan?"

Stefan stood up quickly, caught off-guard. "Y-yes?" he stuttered.

We all leaned forward in our seats, holding our breath. Sam's eyebrows drew together, and he bit his bottom lip. "Are you busy tonight? I mean, would you like to go out . . . with . . . me?"

Stefan was so stunned he grabbed the chair to hold himself up. He nodded, and replied quietly, "That would be great."

Sam's eyes blazed to a brilliant copper, and he blinked to control them. "Good. We should—"

"Make plans," Stefan finished.

"I'll catch up with you—"

"Later this afternoon." He trailed the back of his finger down Sam's bronzed cheek, then left quickly out the garden door. Lowner went to the window to stare after him.

I hopped up from my chair and cried, "You did it! That was so awesome, Sam. Sam? Are you okay?"

He was standing there, blinking slowly. I shook him a little and snapped him out of his trance. A brilliant smile lit his face, and he said, "I've never been this okay in my entire existence. Did I really just do that? And did he say yes?"

"Yes you did, and yes he did," Kirner said. "Maybe the boss has taken the stick out of his ass." Lowner threw a lemon, and it bounced off Kirner's temple. Rubbing the injury, he said, "Come on, Quincy, before your mate kills me. We need to get the plans drawn up for the trip."

"Trip?" Lowner snapped. "What trip?"

Quincy groaned. "I told you about the trip, Low."

"You did not. You never tell me anything."

Greta and Sam took the opportunity to flee. We all knew an explosion was coming. I'd learned early on that whenever Quincy and Lowner started in, it was a long, loud battle. I snuck out and went to the library. I was supposed to be studying recent events, but with the excitement over the dog, and Sam finally making his move, I was too keyed up to study, so I took out my laptop and wasted time by playing games on social media sites. Eventually I drifted off.

I slept until just after noon, when my cell phone rang, jolting me out of an amazing dream about the incredible dexterity of Freyr's tongue. When I looked at the caller ID and saw that it was Greta, I wanted to choke her. "I hate you," I said with a yawn.

She said, "Sorry to hear that, but you have to come out and help us before Stefan sees."

"Help you what?"

"Just get out to the driveway," she commanded.

"Okay, okay. I'm coming."

Still coming out of my nap fog, I was completely confused by the nervous expressions on my friends' faces as I approached.

"Quick," Sam said. "Help us with them."

"Them?" I repeated loudly.

"Shh!" they both hissed. Greta opened the back of the Land Rover and my jaw dropped. Four squirming puppies were rolling around in a large basket. They were big puppies.

"Not that I really want to know," I said, "but are those Great Danes?"

Greta nodded and clapped like a child. "Yes! Aren't they adorable? This one's mine. Her name is Poppy." She retrieved a white dog with large black spots, and squeezed it so tightly I thought it was going to be crushed.

Sam hefted up two puppies. "And these are Ramesses the Great and Nefertari. I'm hoping that Stefan will want to . . . I hope I can keep both, wherever I end up."

I laughed. "You two are insane. Freyr will never allow this."

Greta smiled wickedly and put Poppy onto the grass. Then she produced a gray puppy from the basket and held it up. She shook its paw at me and said in a kid's voice, "Hello, Daddy. Aren't I cute?"

Instant love. Those saggy eyes locked on mine, and I snatched the small canine from Greta. "Aww. He's so adorable. I love him."

Sam set his two down to play with Poppy. "Yours is the runt of the litter."

"And yet he's still huge," I said. "Let's think of a good name for you. What about Titus? That's perfect for my little emperor."

"Is that the dog?" called a voice from behind us. We all jumped and panicked. Stefan's eyes first stopped on Titus, then followed a predictable path to the other three puppies chewing at Greta's sandals. His eyes blazed in fury. "Four?" he bellowed.

Greta put up her hands defensively as though Stefan was about to attack her. "Now, let's not be hasty. Sam and I went up there and they were just so cute that I couldn't decide. Freyr said I could get a dog."

"Yes. A dog. One dog. One, as in singular. Four is not singular!"

In a calculated move, Sam held up the pharaoh and his queen and said, "But aren't they gorgeous? I thought if I . . . you might like her . . . oh, never mind."

Stefan's anger evaporated and we knew he'd been trapped by Sam's invisible hold on him. Stefan smiled and took the puppy. "What's her name?"

"Nefertari," Sam told him.

"What a mouthful." Stefan smirked when Sam's breath caught. He held up the puppy and looked in her eyes. "So how about I call you Neff? You think you could put up with me? What about him?" He pointed to Sam. "I hope so, because Sam and I are a package deal."

Sam's jaw dropped and he began to back away, unable to believe what he'd just heard. His voice trembled when he asked, "What are you saying?"

Stefan took the dogs and thrust them at Greta, who hurried to catch them. Then he pulled Sam's body into his own and said, "I'm saying that I love you. I've never wanted anything else in my life more than I want you. I have for a long time, but I've been too much of a coward to do anything about it. With everything happened lately, I decided I didn't want to wait any longer. I'm sorry for wasting so much time, but will you have me now?"

I swear there were tears in Sam's eyes. He put his arms around his mate's neck and sobbed. "If you're all I ever have in this lifetime, I'd be the luckiest person on earth. I love you too, Stefan."

Their mouths came together gently, as if it was a first kiss for both of them. The tip of Stefan's tongue flicked against Sam's lips, which parted and welcomed him. At the first taste of their mate, both men moaned loudly. A switch had been flipped, and they didn't care who was watching. Stefan shoved Sam against the side of the car—rather roughly, I thought, but Sam certainly didn't mind—and forced his knee between Sam's legs. They ground their obvious erections together and Stefan sucked on Sam's neck. It went on for some minutes, so Greta and I sat down and played with the puppies.

When the two lovers came up for air, Stefan said to us, "We are not to be disturbed unless the fucking world is on fire."

He threw Sam over his shoulder and ran back to the house.

"Holy shit," Greta said as we watched the pair disappear inside.

A few minutes after they went in, the door opened and Lowner came out with Quincy, Kirner, and everyone else from the house — except Stefan and Sam. They walked over to us, scratching their heads and looking dazed. Lowner put his hands on his hips and asked Greta, "What have you done?"

"Whatever do you mean?" she replied with an innocent grin.

Quincy looked back at the house and explained. "Stefan came bursting into the kitchen and told us all that we had to get out of the house. What the hell's going on?"

In answer to his question, a ferocious roar came from inside the house. Lowner turned to run back inside, but I put a hand on his shoulder.

"It's fine. Greta, do you want to tell them?"

She snickered and announced, "Stefan has decided to claim his mate."

Their mouths dropped. McGillun returned from shopping and joined us on the lawn. "Are those *four* puppies?" she cried.

Lowner shushed her. "They're the least of the excitement."

"What?" she asked.

The noises coming from the house got progressively louder, and we shouldn't have listened, but it was impossible not to. After watching the Stefan and Sam show for so long, missing the finale was not an option. When the words finally came, we almost applauded, but Stefan probably would have killed us all if we had.

Sam's voice sounded strained, but was still loud. "Yes, Stefan! Oh, fuck, bite me! Mark me!"

A strangled cry rose up as Stefan roared, "Mine! You're mine. Fuck, your ass is so tight."

Kirner groaned quietly and grimaced. "I cannot hear this. Christ! I'm going to leave for a while. Perhaps for the rest of forever."

"*Eternity,*" Greta corrected with a laugh.

"Whichever is longest." He hurried toward his truck and took off out the driveway, nearly plowing into Freyr's Jag as he did.

Greta and I shoved the puppies back into the Rover and tried to appear innocent. Freyr climbed out of the car and eyed us suspiciously. "What's wrong with all of you?"

I put my arms around his waist and said, "Nothing. Welcome home."

He kissed me, but only superficially. He was concentrating on the others standing there watching the house. "Why are you all out here? Get back inside to work."

"Stefan kicked us out," Lowner said.

"Huh?" Freyr asked. "Why? What's he doing?"

"Sam," Greta said. We all snorted and Freyr growled quietly.

"Carter, explain to me what's going on."

The voices from inside answered for me. "Fuck me, Stefan! I need to taste you!"

"Take my blood, Sam. Be my — holy shit!" His cry was drowned out by Sam's roar as he claimed his mate.

Things finally quieted down, and I wrenched my gaze away from the house to look at Freyr, who was staring toward Stefan's bedroom windows in absolute stupefaction. "When did that happen?" he finally was able to ask.

Greta said, "Right after he saw the dogs — I mean dog. The dog."

Freyr put his hands on his hips. "What do you mean *dogs?*"

She laughed nervously. "Dogs? No. I said dog. Just one."

He looked around her at the Rover, from which came the inharmonious strain of four distinct yips. He opened the door and froze. He picked up two puppies and said, "This is one dog, huh?"

"She's mine," Greta said, pointing to Poppy. "And the gray one is Carter's."

Freyr's breathing changed and he glared at me.

I smiled and said, "Isn't he cute? His name is Titus."

He put Poppy and Titus down and picked up Ramesses and Nefertari. "And these?"

"That's Sam's and the other is Stefan's," I explained.

"*Stefan's?* I'm going to kill him."

Quincy whistled and said, "Sam might just do it for you. Listen."

Stefan's voice was scratchy. "Okay . . . Sam, stop. I'm . . . oh, Jesus, stop, before you kill me."

Freyr was off like a rocket before I could hold him back. "Get back here!" I called to him.

He scaled the wall with ease and broke through the window into Stefan's bedroom. We waited breathlessly for a few seconds before there was an infuriated howl. Freyr came flying back out through the other window, propelled by some force inside the room.

Quincy laughed loudly and said, "They threw him back out. Mother*fucker*, that is a riot."

My seriously pissed-off mate disentangled himself from a rose bush and stalked back toward us, plucking thorns out of his ruined shirt. We all tried not to laugh, but it was impossible. Quincy said, "Pardon me for being blunt, sir, but didn't you recognize the sound of someone sucking cock?"

The threatening growl that came from Freyr killed our laughter. He barked, "Shut the fuck up, Quincy, and figure out how to fix those fucking windows."

Quincy nodded once and made for the barn. Lowner and McGillun pretended to go unload supplies, and Greta and I were left to face Freyr. Smiling sweetly, she reached up to pluck a thorn from his neck.

"Don't even try it!" he yelled. "The two of you can take all four of those things back to wherever you got them. Now."

Greta opened her mouth to protest, but I held a hand up to stop her. "Don't you say a word, Greta. I have no intention of taking the puppies back."

"What did you say?" Freyr barked.

I took a step toward him. "The puppies stay."

"No."

"Yes. Or you can find another place to sleep."

That stopped Freyr dead in his tracks. "Are you blackmailing me?"

"That's exactly what I'm doing. You won't get anything until you promise not to send the puppies back."

His lips curled and he snarled, "Fine. We'll just see which one of us lasts longer."

Shit. He had me cornered and he knew it. Taking a deep breath to kill my hardening cock, I said, "Fine. No kissing, touching, nothing."

"Good. Until then, the puppies go in the barn."

"In the *barn?*" Greta cried.

Freyr leaned down until he was level with her carnation eyes. "Would you like to sleep with them and eat dog food?"

She shook her head meekly, loaded the dogs into the basket and carried it toward the barn, scowling the entire way.

That evening, after those of us who ate food had finished dinner, we all went into the great room to relax and have fun, but the air in the room was so strained that no one was really enjoying themselves. Stefan and Sam had yet to emerge from the bedroom, and Freyr had spent the entire afternoon in his office. He hadn't come to dinner, and I was fuming. He always sat and spent time with me while I ate.

When Freyr finally joined us in the great room thirty

minutes later, the air caught in my throat, and I gripped the arms of the chair with my nails. I'd never seen him dressed as he was that night, and I wanted him so badly my cock immediately sprang to full mast. He'd foregone his usual evening uniform of a polo shirt and jeans in favor of a deep blue, button-up oxford that was perfectly fitted over his hard abs. The top three buttons were undone, which allowed just a hint of his chest to show. The sleeves were rolled back, and I licked my lips at the sight of his muscled forearms. Loose gray dress pants completed the outfit, making my mate the sexiest man I'd ever seen.

When he saw me drooling, an evil grin spread across his face. "Good evening, love."

"Hi," I said curtly.

Freyr surveyed the room. "Has Stefan still not come down?"

"No, sir," Kirner said. "Should we send a search party?"

"Are you insane? I'm still picking thorns out of my butt. Speaking of pains in the ass, are the animals in the barn?"

"Yes," Greta huffed. "How about I get them crates instead?"

"That's a good idea," I replied. "Where would we get them?"

"Well, since they'll have to be pretty big," she said with a sweet grin, "I was hoping to talk to Kirner about it."

Kirner was talking to Quincy. He stopped mid-sentence and asked, "Talk to me about what?"

Greta rubbed her hands on her jeans, seemingly embarrassed at being overheard by him. I knew she had a crush on him, and her confidence disappeared whenever he talked to her. "I was thinking that since you're so good with woodworking and stuff, that maybe you'd make the crates for the puppies."

Kirner snorted and curled his lip up. "For the dogs? I'm far too busy to waste time on something so stupid."

With a trembling lip, Greta left the room. I turned on Kirner and slapped the side of his head.

"What the fuck is wrong with you?" I snapped.

"Excuse me?" Kirner replied. "What was that for?"

"For treating Greta so badly," Freyr said. "That was a shitty thing to say."

"What are you all talking about? All I said was I'm too busy to build dog crates."

I rolled my eyes. "No, that's not what you said. You called it stupid. How do you think that made Greta feel?"

"But it's just Greta."

"Oh my God!" Lowner cried. "Kirner, certainly you're not that dense, are you? She likes you, you idiot."

Kirner just stood there, looking dazed.

"For fuck's sake, he is that dense," Freyr said.

"Wait a minute," Kirner mumbled. "You're trying to tell me that Greta *likes* me?"

"*Yes!*" we all shouted.

"Oh."

"Oh?" I repeated. "That's all you're going to say?"

"I don't know what else to say. How long —"

"Since the day she met you, you imbecile," Lowner snapped.

Freyr had told me Greta's story one day, and I'd listened in horror and sobbed. During the Second World War, an older female vampire named Mazrin, who lived in a small town near Munich, had come upon a group of German soldiers raping a young woman. After killing all of the Nazis attacking the girl, Mazrin brought her into her own home to recover. Her physical wounds had healed, but when Greta discovered two months later she was pregnant, she tried to commit suicide. Again, Mazrin saved her. She explained that if Greta was turned into a vampire, then the fetus would not survive. As grief-stricken as she was, Greta agreed, and the nineteen-year-old girl was changed. After her transition and basic instruction, Mazrin contacted Freyr, saying Greta needed to be educated and given more opportunity than could be provided in a small German village. Stefan and Kirner traveled that week to bring her home.

"Don't you remember, Kirner?" Freyr asked. "How terrified she was of everyone except you? She clung to you whenever anyone came near her, but eventually she gained our trust. You were so wonderful with her, so patient, but you've changed. Why are you that way with her? Don't you care for her?"

"What kind of question is that?" he barked. "Of course I care for her. I care very much for her. But I think she will have a man not from here, not one of us. She thinks of me only as a brother."

"That's not it at all," I explained. "She acts that way because she's nervous you'll reject her—which you've just done."

Kirner winced. "Uh . . . forgive me Herr Amsel, but do you think I could get a few days off? This is just too much. I . . . I don't want her to be uncomfortable around me."

After making sure that all of the posts were covered, Freyr granted Kirner his leave of absence.

Chapter Ten—Carter

That weekend was Greta's ninetieth birthday. We had a huge celebration in the great room, with an enormous red raspberry layer cake, which even Stefan and Freyr ate, at Lowner's insistence. Greta had a blast disemboweling her enormous stack of presents, including a Burberry coat for Poppy from me, and the matching collar and leash from Sam.

The night was a lot of fun, and Greta was buoyant and bubbly, but I could tell that Kirner's absence affected her. His phone was switched off, and his two-day leave of absence had passed. He was now AWOL. Lowner told me Kirner had never missed her birthday in seventy-one years, and everyone wondered what had happened. The night before the party, I'd heard Greta crying in her room. I just wished I could get my hands on the bastard.

Two minutes before midnight, a truck came tearing up the driveway. Stefan's earpiece crackled with static, and he yanked it out with a grimace. A minute later, the door to the hall slammed open and Kirner stood there, panting. Greta's mouth fell open at his sudden appearance. He crossed the room to stand in front of her, with his hands in his pockets, looking embarrassed.

"Where were you?" she asked quietly.

"At my cabin, in the north."

"What cabin?" Freyr blurted out. I kicked him in the shin to shut him up.

Kirner ignored us both. "I am sorry it took such a long time. I wanted very much to finish your present."

"M-my present?"

Kirner beamed. "Just wait here. Quincy, will you help bring it in?"

Lowner grumbled something like, "Always, my mate," but Quincy patted him on the head and went to help retrieve the gift. They brought back an enormous crate, almost five feet high, four feet wide and several feet long.

Greta shook with excitement. "What is it?" she asked. "Lemme see!"

"I hope you like it," Kirner said, removing screws with his drill. The sides of the crate fell away, and Lowner whimpered at the gouges in the floor.

The rest of us didn't notice, though. We were all staring in amazement at the enormous doghouse Kirner had crafted. It was styled like an English country cottage, complete with window boxes that held food and water dishes, and a mailbox with Poppy's name on it.

"Oh my God," Sam muttered. We all nodded in agreement.

Kirner exhaled slowly, and showed off the dog's new piece of real estate. "If you lift the side of the roof, there's space for collars and toys. The bottom slides out for easy cleaning, and the wires can been taken out of the windows when she doesn't need to be in the crate anymore."

He looked hopefully at Greta, who was staring at him without moving a muscle. It was getting tense for a moment, until Greta finally flung herself at Kirner. "Thank you," she said, putting her arms around his neck. "I really love it." Without letting go, she pushed up on her toes and pressed her lips to his. Then she pulled her head back, gasped in horror, and bolted out the French doors and across the lawn.

None of us moved. The only sound in the room was that of the puppies playing on the carpet. Kirner stood there for a minute, thunderstruck at what had happened. Then, he touched his finger to his lips and took off after her.

"Do you promise you won't send the puppies back?" I struck a pose, one hand on my hip.

Freyr was struggling to get his pants off. He looked up with them wrapped around his feet. "I promise I will not send the puppies back. Can I please fuck you now?"

My cock throbbed from pent-up lust. Freyr and I hadn't laid a finger on each other for four days. Everyone in the house knew about the "bet" and had been very careful to avoid upsetting either one of us during our celibacy. After the birthday party, however, we couldn't resist anymore. So there I stood in our bedroom, wearing nothing except Freyr's tie.

"Do you really want to fuck me?" I pulled the tie off slowly, then wrapped it around my cock. I held his gaze while I stroked it softly.

"Oh, shit," Freyr groaned. His voice was more like a croak at that point, and the fact that I had such an effect on him made my heart race. I was just as worked up as he was, and it took all of my willpower to keep my dick from exploding while I performed.

A drop of pre-cum gathered on my cock, and I wiped it off with my finger. Then I sucked it into my mouth with an exaggerated, "*Mm . . .*"

A strange gurgling sound came from Freyr. He ripped his pants to shreds to get free of them, and then tackled me on the bed. Fisting his hands into my hair, he yanked just a little and said, "You better not try to blackmail me again, you little tease."

"Yes, Freyr," I replied with a rumbling purr. I took hold of his hand and licked the inside of his wrist.

He kissed the outer shell of my ear and whispered, "You can smell my blood flowing under this pale skin, can't you? You only need to bite to take what's yours."

I moaned and pierced the offered arm with my fangs. A

sweet rush of blood covered my lips, and I sucked hard at the wound. I collected another drop of liquid from my cock, then offered my finger to Freyr. He licked it, nipped and scratched my skin with his fangs, but then quickly switched his grip and bit my wrist. We'd never fed from each other at the same time before. The experience was so incredible that after a moment, we broke apart, panting. I stuck my tongue out to clean Freyr's blood off my lip, but he shook his head.

"Let me," he said quietly.

"Your own blood?" I asked in surprise. "Are you sure?"

He nodded and touched the tip of his tongue to my mouth. Just the few drops there were enough for him to get a good buzz. I was curious to see how he'd act while hopped up on his own blood, so I held his bleeding wrist up. With a grin, he sank his fangs into his own flesh and sucked. Just one good mouthful was enough to give the full effect.

He muttered, "That *is* good, isn't it?" and then slumped over onto the bed. He seemed to be asleep, mumbling under his breath.

I sat up, completely ape-shit. "What the fuck? He's just going to leave me like this? I don't fucking believe it. Talk about a lightweight."

Suddenly, a loud growl rumbled up from his chest, and he pulled me on top of him. He bit his lip trying not to laugh, but couldn't quite stop himself. He snorted, and I pounded my fist on his chest.

"Ow," he whined. "You're such a brute."

"Asshole," I snapped.

"No, *your* asshole. That's what I want, so hand it over."

It was my turn to stifle my laughter and I just barely succeeded. "How come you're not hallucinating or anything?"

"I feel really good, yes, but not high. Because my body is so much older than yours, I have a higher tolerance for foreign substances. It's sort of like an eighteen-year-old kid's alcohol tolerance versus that of man of fifty. Now, get this amazingly sexy, perfect handful of ass onto my dick."

Freyr was getting lewd and loud, and I loved it. I grabbed the lube, and when I touched him with my slippery fingers, we both nearly lost it. While he held my cheeks apart, I reached back and held the tip of his cock against my hole. With a breathy, "I love you, Freyr," I slid all the way onto him.

"I love you too," he said. "I missed this ass so much. I've been hard as a rock this whole time. I haven't slept in four days."

"You haven't masturbated?" I asked.

He looked at me as if I'd accused him of starting the plague. "And you have?"

The truth was I'd jacked off twice every day that Freyr had slept in a different room. I tried to sound confident when I said, "No. Of course not. Not at all."

"You did," he said. "You're the worst liar. Well, fuck it, then. I'm not going to coddle you. I want you on your hands and knees now."

I'd gotten used to Freyr being dominant once in a while, and I loved it, because he always stopped if I was uncomfortable. I'd agreed to use a safeword if I needed to, so I always had a choice in how far we went.

He entered me again, but only a few inches. I tried to push back against him, but he had a strong hold on my hips. Over and over, he teased me until I was sobbing with need.

"Please, please. Give me more."

He put his hands on my shoulders and thrust into me as deep as he could go. It was a struggle not to lose my balance. He withdrew slowly and slammed in again. The sound of his hips striking my ass made my cock ache, and I could feel myself getting close.

"I can smell you," he said. "Come for me, Carter. Come hard."

"Oh holy . . ."

I felt my dick pulse, and my balls drew up. Freyr wrapped his fingers around me and milked me as I shook and screamed into my pillow. When I clenched my muscles, trying to keep my orgasm going as long as I could, Freyr moaned very loudly. He shuddered against my back, and I felt him come deep within. We fell asleep with Freyr still buried inside me. As I drifted, I heard the puppies barking downstairs. I smiled.

When I woke the next morning, there was a note from Freyr on my nightstand:

Good morning, my love,

I had to go into the city early this morning and didn't want to wake you. Actually, I did want to wake you and fuck you until you brought the walls down, but I took pity on your ass and instead made use of your shower gel. Probably not such a good idea now that I think about it. Knowing that my dick smells like you will undoubtedly keep me hard all day.

Here are a few pages from my journals that I think you'll find very informative. I wasn't sure if I should give them to you or not, but you need to know what really happened.

Rest today, if possible, because tonight I am going to work your ass so hard you won't be able to sit down for a week. I love you. — F

Underneath the note was a folio containing several decaying pieces of parchment. I took them to the library and carefully laid them out on the desk. My jaw dropped when I saw what the document was—Freyr's account of what happened in Drubich and Berlin. I locked myself in the library and poured over the journals, immersing myself in the life of Secundus von Drubich.

I wasn't sure what to think when I finished reading. I was heartbroken for Freyr, for having experienced something so unthinkably horrible, but as upset as I was for him, I was also disconcerted by his fear of Alder. The fact that my mate was so afraid of his brother petrified me. I'd always thought Freyr to be invincible. I assumed if he ever confronted Alder, my mate would have no problem killing him. Now I wasn't so sure.

CHAPTER ELEVEN—CARTER

The night after her birthday party, Greta and Kirner went on their first date. They went to see a movie. When they hadn't come back by 11:30, Freyr began pacing back and forth in the great room, stopping every few minutes to look out the window.

"Where are they?" he grumbled.

Stefan laughed. "Do you realize how ridiculous you look? They're big kids now, time to let go."

"He's right, babe," I said. "You're going to wear a hole in the carpet."

Lowner gasped and said, "That is seventeenth-century Persian. Get off."

He pushed Freyr onto the sofa and bent down to inspect the damage. Quincy came up behind him and mimed screwing his mate like a cowboy riding a bronco, complete with twirling lasso. We all lost it, and Lowner straightened. He glared at Quincy, but before he could start yelling, Greta's car pulled in the drive. Freyr rushed to the window. Naturally, we all followed.

"It's about time," he barked.

"Shh," I scolded.

Kirner climbed out of the sleek little BMW and walked around to open Greta's door. He offered his hand and pulled her quickly out of the car. She landed flat up against him, and she craned her neck to look into his eyes. Kirner said something, and then put an arm around her waist. I wanted him to hurry up and kiss her, but I didn't say anything.

Unfortunately, my mate did.

As Kirner leaned down and brought his mouth to Greta's, Freyr blurted out, "What's he doing?"

The couple outside froze, then turned to see us watching them. Kirner let his hand drop, gave Greta a little wave, and hurried toward his rooms above the stables. Greta glared at us and stalked toward the French doors at the end of the great room. We all backed up, leaving Freyr to face the pissed-off pixie all by himself. She pushed the doors open and stood on the threshold, arms crossed, foot tapping.

Freyr cleared his throat and smiled. "Did you have a good time?"

Greta approached him slowly. "Why yes, *Dad*, we did."

"Good. Why don't—"

"Of course, it would've been a hell of a lot better if you hadn't yelled out your new catchphrase. God damn it! What is wrong with you?" Her scream could carry to Poughkeepsie if she really tried, so in a confined space, it was deafening. We all winced and covered our ears.

"Greta, please stop yelling," I said.

"Sorry," she lied, "but I can't believe you—all of you, watching me like I'm a teenager. It's so humiliating."

Quincy shrugged and said, "Technically you still are a teenager. Nineteen is—"

She leveled a stony gaze at him and growled. "If you don't can it, Quincy, I'm gonna sauté your balls for breakfast." He crossed his legs and Greta turned back to Freyr. "What the hell do you want from me? Every time I want to take a step away from this place, you lock me in."

"So don't let him," I told her. "You're an adult. Go get what you want. God knows you've waited long enough."

Freyr hung his head. "He's right. Jeez, Greta. I'm sorry, I really am. It's just—you're like a daughter to me, and I get . . . protective. I had to wait ten years for Carter, so I can imagine that seventy-one years has been hell."

She slumped onto a sofa. "Actually, it's been seventy years, six months, four days and" — she checked her watch — "about eight hours."

I sat down and put a supportive arm around her shoulder. She drew a shuddering breath and continued. "My family was very poor, and my father beat me and my mother a lot. One night, I'd had enough of him, and snuck out of my room. I wanted to get as far away from him as I could get, but it didn't take long before the patrol caught me.

I was so scared. I knew I was pretty, and I knew from their expressions what they wanted. There were four of them, so it was impossible to fight them off. The first time, the pain made me want to die. After that, I kind of went numb. I just closed my eyes and hoped they'd kill me."

Sam shook his head in disbelief. "My God, I could never imagine what you went through, Greta."

"When the fourth one was on me, the most terrifying growl came from the woods. It was dark, so we couldn't see what it was. The soldiers were scared, too. They'd taken their pistols off while they were with me, and before they had time to reach their weapons, a woman walked out of the woods. She was older, probably fifty, but so beautiful! Everyone knew about vampires, because of what Alder did at the Berlin Museum, but I never expected to see a vampire face to face."

"The Nazis must have been scared shitless," Quincy said.

Greta nodded. "She rushed at them so fast I couldn't follow her movements. Within seconds, they were all dead, lying there on the ground in a bloody heap. I thought I was next, but she sat next to me and put her jacket around my shoulders. She told me her name was Mazrin, she was a nurse, and she would help me."

"A nurse?" I asked.

"Many of the watchers helped the allies during the war,"

Freyr explained. "One pissed-off vampire could take out a lot of the enemy before they could fire a shot. Mazrin was especially effective due to her . . . sex appeal."

"Yeah. Horny soldiers didn't stand a chance against a pair of tits like hers."

Everyone turned to stare at Stefan. He cleared his throat. "So I was told . . . at the time. I mean . . . shit."

Sam's eyes flashed, and he shook with anger. He rose from his seat next to Stefan and went to sit on the chaise on the other side of the room. Stefan rolled his eyes and muttered an apology, which Sam ignored.

"So you went with Mazrin?" I asked Greta.

"There wasn't much of a choice. If I'd been found next to four dead officers, I would've been shot on sight. She took me to a tiny stone cottage and took care of me. That was the first time someone had cared for me like that. After she changed me, she began teaching me everything she could, but it wasn't a lot during the war. One day she told me I was going to America to live with some other vampires, and I freaked out. I didn't want to go anywhere, especially with men. She was the only family I knew. Then Stefan showed up. He was huge and intimidating, but he was so kind. It was the first time in my life a man had been nice to me. He brought me the most beautiful dresses, and a warm coat and shoes. It was my first pair of new shoes."

"Is that why you have over a hundred pairs of them now?" Lowner asked.

She ignored him and continued. "I'd never celebrated Christmas before, but I remember thinking it must be like that."

I stopped her and asked, "Stefan, what you do, smuggle that stuff in?"

"Yes," he said bluntly, as though he didn't understand my surprise. "She was so tiny and frightened, clutching Mazrin's hand. And then Kirner came in."

Greta smiled shyly. "He was my hero, my knight in shining armor who came to take me away to his castle. He got down on his knees so I didn't have to look up to see his face, then he asked me my name. From the minute I heard his voice, he became the center of my world."

"That is so sweet," I gushed.

"It was hard to leave Mazrin, but Stefan took a photograph of her and me, and said he'd help me write letters. Then Kirner helped me into the car and I didn't feel quite so afraid. The whole way to Switzerland, he told me about traveling by plane, listening to music on the radio, the cinema. He had even brought me a copy of Look Magazine. It was in English, so I couldn't read it—hell, I could barely read German—but it nearly disintegrated from me flipping the pages back and forth, looking at the pictures."

Freyr said, "When you got here, everything was new to you. We had so much fun showing you around."

"The bathtub." Lowner laughed. "McGillun didn't think she'd ever get you out of it."

We all laughed, and she shrugged. "I loved baths and Hershey bars."

"Hershey bars?" Sam asked.

Lowner snorted. "She ate about a pound of chocolate a week, and Freyr insisted we indulge her. Do you know how hard it was to find that much chocolate during the war? It's a good thing she's cute."

Quincy teased, "It's a good thing she can't gain weight. Otherwise, she'd be a blimp."

Greta gave him the finger, and he blew her a kiss. She continued, "It was so wonderful. I learned to speak English, and to read and write. The whole time, Kirner was right there, helping me get used to the whole immortality thing, but then he started spending less time with me. As I got more comfortable here, he became more distant. He was always busy, always volunteering for some trip to God-knows-where. At first, when he got back from a job, he'd talk to me about where he'd been and things, but eventually, he didn't even do that, so I just kind of gave up. I thought he didn't want me around anymore."

"I have always wanted you around." We all turned to see Kirner in the doorway. Greta's eyes grew wide when she realized she'd been overheard. I stood, and Kirner took my place on the sofa. He held her hand and explained. "Greta, there is nothing I like more than to be with you, but you had not been around other people than us. I did not want you to choose me just because there was no one else. So I pushed you away, to make you meet other . . . oh, I do not know what I tried to do. I'm sorry I have not told you for so long. I want to be with you, if you want that."

She blinked twice and then smiled. "Of course I do, you dope."

Kirner put a hand under her chin and kissed her very gently and carefully. She gave us all the evil eye, so we turned as one and fled the room.

Freyr practically dragged me upstairs. I turned to go toward our room, but he went in the opposite direction.

"Oof!" I grunted when he yanked my arm. "Where are we going?"

"Shh!"

"But where—"

He stopped suddenly, and I crashed into the back of him. "Carter, what part of *shh!* do you not comprehend?"

"Bully."

His jaw tightened, and he raised an eyebrow. I clasped my hands not so innocently behind my back, tilted my hips out and ran my tongue slowly over my fangs. Freyr's breathing came faster and he moved toward me, but then he remembered his original purpose and continued down the hall. Halfway down the east wing, he reached behind a huge Grecian amphora and pressed a button on the wall behind it. A piece of the wood-paneled wall slid open to reveal a modern keypad.

The code was twelve digits long. After he entered the numbers, I heard a muted click. An entire section of the wall opened into a two-foot wide, five-foot high door. The light from the hall barely penetrated the first few feet.

I opened my mouth to say something, but Freyr anticipated me. Without looking back at me, he slapped his hand over my mouth. We climbed in, and he shut the door. Utter darkness pushed painfully on my chest. I'd always hated the dark, especially since Alder had kept me locked up so frequently. But this wasn't Alder. This was my mate, who loved me, so I brought my breathing under control.

Freyr ruffled my hair. "Now we can talk, brat. Just don't move."

Like an idiot, I stepped backward and said, "I really don't like the d-daaark!" as the floor fell out from under me. I tumbled down a stone spiral staircase, banging my head with every flip, until I finally got my bearings and grabbed a step with my hands.

"Son of a bitch!" I cried. "I think I'm bleeding."

"Yummy," purred Freyr from above.

"Not a time to be cute, asshole."

"Sorry. Can you see anything?"

"Besides my life flashing before my eyes? It's pitch-fucking-black down here!"

"Stop yelling and use your eyes."

"Oh, right," I shot back. "Let's see. Yup. There are two mangled legs and—uh oh. I only have one arm now. Is the other one up there?"

"I'm going to wallop you if you don't cut it out."

"Ha! You'll have to find me first." Instantly, he was directly in front of me, and I jumped back in surprise. I looked to where I thought his face must be and saw his eyes blazing orange. I gasped at his appearance. "Dude, your eyes are glowing."

"Dude, so are yours. Now focus."

I blinked a few times and tried to focus on him. His features slowly became clearer, as though a dimmed light bulb was growing brighter. "Cool!" I exclaimed. "I have night vision."

"You're so easily amused. Now, come on."

"How much farther? I feel like I just dropped two floors."

"We're heading into the sub-basement."

"Why are the stairs to the sub-basement on the second floor? Kinda counterintuitive, isn't it?"

"When the house was built, before we moved here, this passage was used for smuggling. No one ever thought to look for secret stashes on the second floor. They always assumed the hidden rooms would be on the first floor. To confuse them, the smugglers built a few dummy tunnels off the first floor and used this as the real entrance. When I bought the place and found the door, I had it secured."

"What did they smuggle?" I asked, not sure if I wanted to know the answer.

"A lot of things."

"Slaves?"

"Possibly, or rum. But enough of that. Come with me."

"I thought you'd never ask."

I grabbed his ass, and he swatted my hand away. "Are you ever not horny?"

"Around you, alone, in the dark?"

"Later." He gave me a quick kiss then turned to continue down the stairs. At the bottom, we came to a large wooden door. Freyr opened it and flipped a light switch. Fluorescent lights buzzed and blinked to life and illuminated a large storage room. After my eyes adjusted, I stood and stared. This wasn't any old, musty basement. On one end sat several large pieces of furniture covered with white sheets. There were shelves upon shelves of boxes, with labels in German and French. One cabinet overflowed with silver, another with pewter, and another was alarmingly full of delicate porcelain. Every available inch of wall space was hung with paintings from the Renaissance, which was Freyr's favorite. I studied a charming little Madonna and Child painted by Botticelli, then realized that he'd probably bought it from . . . Botticelli. I shivered.

Freyr put his arm around my waist. "So what do you think?"

"I think you have one hell of a mess on your hands. Where did it all come from?"

"After five hundred years, you tend to have quite a collection."

"Right," I said sheepishly. "At least it looks like everything's preserved well."

"The room is climate-controlled, so that isn't an issue. There's just so much of it, and we've had no one to catalogue and organize it properly. That's where you come in."

"Me?"

He shrugged. "You were talking about some sort of task to keep you busy. Well, here's your mission, if you choose to accept it — to organize and catalogue every bit of my collection into some sort of database or something."

I exhaled slowly, studying the massive space. There were more paintings in flat crates against the walls, and I itched to see what they were. It would be quite a job, but it would also be a history lesson — a look into Freyr's past. I jumped at the chance.

"Of course I want to do it, but since I'm not up on

computers, could I maybe have Sam help me? Apparently, he's a little bit of a hacking phenom."

"Sure," Freyr replied. "Stefan said Sam's restless and bored. You and he will have to do all your own research, though. You can't get any outside help, or bring anything out of the house."

"Why not?"

"Some of these pieces are unknown works by famous artists. If people found out what I have in here, we'd be inundated by art historians and collectors, clamoring to buy the collection. No, everything stays here. If anything needs cleaning or restoration, I have a trusted friend who will come here. If furniture needs to be fixed, Kirner will do that."

I nodded in acquiescence, and began to poke around a stack of fine porcelain dinner plates. Freyr took me by the shoulders and said, "Another thing, because I know you so well."

"What?"

He scowled. "Titus is not to enter this room."

"But he'll be lonely without his daddy."

Freyr barked out a laugh. "May I remind you, sweetheart, that our son—as you so annoyingly call him—spends most of the day in the kitchen with his partners in canine crime, gobbling up all the treats that Lowner thinks we don't know he gives them? Titus is going to weigh eight hundred pounds."

"Okay." I pouted and tucked my hips into Freyr's. I rolled them side to side, letting him feel just how much I wanted him.

He cleared his throat and said, "Down, boy."

With a laugh, I took a step back and adjusted my jeans. Then I looked around at the clutter. "Where should I start? This is room is at least, what . . . five hundred square feet?"

"Roughly, but there are four more rooms through those doors on the left."

"Well it's a good think I'm immortal, 'cause this is going to take for-fucking-ever."

Freyr snickered. "I'll pay you in sexual favors."

"You certainly have a way with words, Casanova." I backed up to the wall and pulled him against me.

"Let me take you upstairs," he said, nuzzling into my throat.

"No. Take me right here." I dropped to my knees and pushed his pants down. His boxers were next, and his erection bounced up and caught me in the chin.

"Oh, I like the way you think," he mumbled.

I slicked my tongue around the head of his cock. The sweet taste was second only to his blood in the way my body reacted. I wrapped my hands around the base and swallowed as much of him as I could. He gasped and put a hand on the back of my head. The other was braced against the wall.

Sucking my mate's cock was one of my favorite things to do. I moaned, and the vibrations in my throat made his balls draw up close to his body. Just before he was about to come, I backed off, much to Freyr's annoyance. He was happy, though, when I turned around, shoved my pants down around my knees and said, "Fuck me, baby."

There was no preparation before he entered me in one hard push. I bit my lip to contain my yelp of surprise, but then I let my mouth drop open in a loud groan of pleasure. His hands were on the door on either side of my head, and he grunted with each bruising thrust.

"I love you so fucking much, Carter," he said. "Damn, your ass is tight when I take you like this."

I clenched my cheeks together and reveled in the moan my action drew from Freyr. He sped up his thrusts and pierced my neck with his fangs. As he drank, he reached around and pumped my dick.

"Don't . . . stop." The feeling of his cock inside me, his lips and tongue gliding over my sensitive skin plus his warm fingers squeezing me was enough to send me over the edge. I grabbed his other hand and bit his wrist.

He cried out and slammed me flat into the wall as he filled my ass. I came all over my stomach and the door. With a slow sweep of my tongue, I closed the bite on Freyr's wrist. He did the same to my shoulder and we stood there panting, still connected. After a few minutes, Freyr pulled out and I chuckled.

"Damn," I muttered.

"Feeling's mutual," he replied.

After an intense kiss, we straightened our clothes and went back upstairs. Stefan was in the hall when we emerged. He looked at us and scowled. Lifting his wrist up to his mouth, he spoke into his com device. "Matt, will you wipe the footage from the sub-basement for the last half-hour? Thanks." He went on past us, but then turned at the end of the hall to say, "By the way, Carter, your fly's undone, and Freyr, you have blood on your chin. Must've been a good time."

Chapter Twelve—Carter

The next morning, I was walking on clouds. Well, more like sleeping on them, since I was wrapped up like a cocoon in my down comforter. Freyr had let me sleep in, and I could feel it was going to be a good day. I checked the clock and saw that it was a quarter past ten, so I dragged my ass into the bathroom and showered.

Just as I was pulling on my sweater, the door burst open and Freyr rushed at me. The wild look in his eyes scared me, and I backed away.

"Come on," he said, holding his hand out for me.

I took it and said, "What's wrong, Freyr?"

"There's not time to explain right now. I just want you safe. Hurry up."

"Freyr, you're scaring me."

He stopped and kissed my forehead. "I'm going to take care of you, love. But right now, I need you to stay with Sam and Greta, and don't come out until I say so."

We turned down the hall to Greta's bedroom and I gasped. Twelve armed guards in black BDUs were standing outside of her door. Sam and Greta were already there, huddled on the bed.

"What's all of this about?" Greta asked. "Where's Kirner?"

Freyr ignored her and spoke to the guards. "I want six of you outside these windows. Six in the hall. No one gets in this room except for Stefan, Kirner, or me. Understood?"

"Yes, sir," they all replied.

He gave me another quick kiss. "I love you, Carter. It'll be all right." Then he turned to the guards and said, "Orders are to kill on sight." I gasped and my chest constricted. This was deathly serious. He shut the door and we heard him say, "If anything happens to these three, I'll have your heads."

Greta was shaking with fear. "What the fuck? Carter, he didn't tell you what was going on?"

"No. Nothing. I'm so freaked out."

Sam spoke up. "I heard Stefan say they found a connection to the woman in your room, and when the guard said the name — which I couldn't hear — he went nuts. He brought me down here, and that was it."

I wrapped my arms around my knees. "If they've put this much security on the three of us, it must be really bad."

For two excruciating hours we held each other on her bed, trying to act normal and watch TV, but not really succeeding. Finally one of the guards opened the door and Kirner came in. Greta ran to him, and he hugged her fiercely. His jaw quivered as he said, "Come on, all of you."

The group in the kitchen included Freyr and Stefan, as well as most of the guard. I didn't see Lowner at first, but then noticed him sobbing in the corner, clasped tightly to Quincy's chest. Freyr was staring into space, clearly upset by what had happened. I sat right next to him, and he took my hand. He kissed the top of my head and said, "I'm not going to sugar-coat things. About a week ago, we located the footage of the woman who stole Carter's blood supply from the clinic. Once we found her, we looked through the security feeds and were able see the tags on her car. We put her under surveillance, but she didn't really do anything out of the ordinary, until last . . . last night."

Stefan took over, as Freyr seemed too upset to continue. "Last night, our surveillance team witnessed the woman meet with someone from our clan."

"What?" I breathed. "You can't be serious. Who?"

Freyr looked in my eyes. "McGillun."

Greta shrieked in surprise. To hear that the only other female in the house was a traitor pushed her off the deep end.
"No. She wouldn't do that. You're wrong, Stefan. You have to
be wrong." Kirner pinned her arms to her sides to keep her
from attacking Stefan. She kicked and sobbed until she finally
wore herself out.

I was so horrified that I didn't know what to say or think.
We sat in silence for a long while, until I asked, "Why?"

Stefan said, "Apparently, Alder approached McGillun
shortly after he'd attacked your family. Once he realized
you'd survived your suicide attempt, he wanted to get you
back. He figured the easiest way to get information would be
to find the weakest link in our clan and exploit it. McGillun
was an easy target. Somehow he charmed her, and made her
think he loved her."

"I don't believe it," Sam mumbled.

"We can't corroborate that," Stefan replied, "but he definitely used her to get information. How she managed to keep
up her charade with us for so long I'll never know."

The way he said those words made me feel ill. I turned to
Freyr. "Where is she now?"

One look into his guilt-ridden eyes was all it took. McGillun was dead. My mate had killed her—executed her. Without answering my question, he got up and walked out the
back door. I followed him to the far corner of the garden.

He started speaking before I could ask any questions. "It
was so easy. That's what bothers me the most. When I found
out she'd betrayed us, put you in so much danger, all of the
feeling went out of my body. I didn't comprehend what I was
doing. I could see I was hurting her, making her bleed, but I
didn't care. I've never felt that kind of rage."

I fell to my knees and dry-heaved while he described
McGillun's death. He shrugged. "It didn't take long before

she told us everything. After that, Stefan and I agreed that we couldn't let her go."

"Did you kill her, or did Stefan?" I asked.

He turned to look at me. "I did. It was very quick, and she even asked me to forgive her."

"And did you forgive her?"

He reached out his hand and helped me to my feet. Then he answered quietly, "No."

After a few days went by and the shock wore off, Freyr called us all into the great hall. He wouldn't tell me what it was about, and when he began talking, I could see why.

"In light of what's happened, our plans for the trip to Germany have changed. Quincy and his team will remain here with Greta, Sam, and Carter. Stefan, Kirner, and will I take a small —"

"No way!" I cried. "I'm not sitting here while you go hunting for Alder. Forget it."

Freyr sighed. "You're not coming. It's too dangerous."

I shook with anger. "Have you forgotten I'm a vampire now? I can take care of myself, asshole."

Sam stood. "If any of Alder's clan has used an electronic device in the last ten years, I can find them. So, I'm going." Stefan opened his mouth to say something, but Sam stopped him with a dead-cold stare. "Stefan, if you say anything right now, I'll strangle you! Everyone here thinks that Carter, Greta, and I are helpless little children. You practically dictate to us when to eat, when to sleep, when we can go out. Freyr, did you know your mate hasn't been outside the gates since he came here?"

The truth was I'd forgotten about the outside world. Apparently, so had Freyr. He looked horrified and stuttered, "W-well, I —"

"No, you didn't," Sam snapped back. "How are we

supposed to survive locked up in this house, worried sick that the demented, sadistic fuck of a brother of yours might be waiting for you to leave, so he can come in here and slaughter us? Or maybe he's in Germany now, lying in wait, just hoping you'd be dumb enough to try and attack. Better yet, maybe he's in Fiji, sampling the local flavors while he watches us running around with our heads up our asses. Jesus Christ! Will you please let us help you?"

Sam won the argument.

CHAPTER THIRTEEN—CARTER

"Greta, will you please see my reasons?"

I heard her snort. "No, but I'll *listen* to reason."

"Stop correcting my English," Kirner shot back.

"Your Eng-ulsh?"

"My In-gu-lish!"

She cackled. "That's even worse."

"I am not finding this funny."

"*Entschuldigung.*"

"*Mein Gott,* you are driving me crazy."

"Well, at least it'll be a short trip."

At that point, I was trying so hard not to laugh, I felt light-headed. Sam clutched his gut and breathed heavily through his nose. We'd been standing outside Greta's bedroom door for the last five minutes, listening to the argument. Kirner sounded like he was ready to strangle her.

"That's it. You're not going," he said.

"Like hell I'm not."

"You do not take things seriously, Greta. This trip will be very dangerous, and if you cannot behave, then I will not bring you."

"But you like it when I don't behave."

Sam raised an eyebrow, and I waggled my hips back and forth. He gave me the finger for making him laugh, and we turned back to listen at the door.

"You are always with the jokes. No. I will not be worrying about you the whole trip."

"Anything I can do to change your mind?"

"No."

"What about this?"

Kirner's voice was slightly unstable. "D-do not think that using your body will change my . . . holy mother of . . ."

Sam and I looked at each other in amusement. Greta was using the oldest trick in the book. I was jealous of how quickly her plan worked, though. "You like this one?" she asked him. "What about if I just take it off?"

"No. Don't take . . . oh, those are so perfect. Come here."

She chuckled. "I don't want to come there. I want to come on the bed. At least the first time."

Kirner choked and spluttered in response. My jaw dropped. Sam's face wore a similar expression, but neither one of us moved. It was completely pervy to stand there and listen, but it was like a train wreck—we couldn't walk away. We heard the rustle of clothes being removed, and I couldn't help but imagine what Kirner's hard body would look like.

"Are you thirsty?" Greta asked breathlessly. I knew she hadn't fed Kirner yet, so I wasn't surprised by his hesitation.

"What? Of course . . . are you sure?"

"Sweetie, I've been waiting over seventy years for this, and so have you."

I heard the bed creak. "Greta, do you know how much I love you?"

"Show me," she said quietly. After a few seconds, her heart rate went through the roof, and I smelled fresh blood. She cried out, "Oh my God! Mmm . . . I love you too."

There was a low growl, and quiet whimpers and laughs flowed from the room. Sam looked at me, and we both grinned with excitement for our friend. She'd finally won the happiness she deserved so much.

I was so giddy I accidentally brushed against the wall and knocked a large framed engraving off its hook. It fell to the floor and the glass shattered, making a noise loud enough to wake the dead. Unfortunately, it startled Sam and me so much that we froze to the spot, instead of fleeing the scene.

Stefan came running down the hall, a look of panic on his face. Lowner — who could hear a mess being made anywhere within a five mile radius — charged up the back stairs from the kitchen, one hand clutching his chest, the other holding a broom and dustpan. Freyr arrived soon after.

"What are you two doing?" he barked. I made a mental note to give the man a list of alternatives to that question.

From inside the room, Greta roared, "For the love of Christ! Carter, Sam, I'm going to fucking kill you two. Freyr, and Stefan and Lowner, since I have no doubt you're out there as well — I'll give a pass to since it's your first offense. you're next. Now will you please all get the fuck away from my door and go make the arrangements for your funerals."

Lowner took the frame and the large pieces of glass, and ran. I tried to run, as did Sam, but our mates literally took us by the collars and dragged us to the office. We were thrust into chairs in front of Freyr's desk. He put his hands flat on the blotter and leaned toward us, jaw clenched. Stefan stood behind him, feet set apart and hands clasped behind his back, with no expression whatsoever, therefore making him fuckloads more frightening than Freyr.

I knew they were waiting for me to start explaining, but I wasn't going to fall for that shit. Neither was Sam. When we remained intelligently silent, Freyr sighed. "You can relax, guys. I think Greta's the one to fear at the moment. But the voyeurism has to stop."

"It's not our hobby!" I snapped. Then hurried through the rest of my flimsy excuse without stopping for breath. "I was going to take Sam down to the storage rooms, because he really wanted to see them, but when we went past Greta's door we sort of heard them talking and stuff, and it was just kinda too tempting not to listen, so we got caught up in everything.

And then I bumped against the wall and knocked the print off, and by the way was it a really valuable print?"

It took Freyr a second to realize I'd stopped talking and had asked him a question. He stuttered, "Uh . . . y-yes. Albrecht Dürer, 1513."

My stomach hurt. "Is it ruined?

"Probably not."

"Maybe I should call the restorer and have it looked at."

"Yes, that would be—God damn it. Don't change the subject. This is exactly why I have such reservations about the two of you coming to Germany."

Sam laughed. "That's the same thing Kirner said to Greta." Stefan raised an eyebrow, and Sam's smile evaporated.

Freyr said, "I need to know you two are ready to make this trip. Trust me, Stefan and I both want you there with us. Being separated from our mates, and not knowing you'll be all right, will make us all much more vulnerable."

"So," Stefan said, "we've decided to give you two a little instruction on how to defend yourselves. There's a lot to go over, and we don't have much time, so I've set up a schedule of sixteen hours training, two hours rest, sixteen training, two rest, etc."

Our jaws dropped. I cried, "That's inhuman!"

Stefan's grin was evil. "It's a good thing you're not *human* anymore, isn't it? Go and rest up. We start at 0600 hours. Oh, and wear clothes you don't mind getting muddy. It rained this afternoon."

He and Freyr walked out. Sam looked at me and said, "We are so fucked."

At 0600 hours—or six a.m. for people without poles shoved up their asses—Sam and I trudged across the lawn toward the training area.

"I'm sorry," I said miserably.

Sam laughed. "What for? Didn't you hear our mates say they want us to come with them? Be happy."

My heart lightened somewhat until I saw Greta approaching. "Cover your balls," I whispered.

But she didn't seem angry. She said simply, "I have to apologize to you two."

"To us?" I asked.

"Yeah. You see, mine isn't the only bedroom with a thin door. I eavesdrop on you guys a lot, and let me tell you, I'm impressed. If Freyr's dick is as big as you say it is, Carter, I'm surprised you can walk. And Sam?" She suddenly flattened her body against the front of his. While he stood there stunned, she wound her fingers in his hair. My jaw dropped, and I wondered what the fuck would happen if Stefan or Kirner saw what she was doing. She pulled his head down and whispered in his ear, "You are one kinky boy, aren't you?" With a wink, she let him go and continued toward the house. A sweet tinkle of laughter floated in her wake.

"What the hell was that about?" I asked. He ignored my question, and I noticed him adjust his pants. I gasped. "Do you have an erection?"

He stopped and looked at me. "A eunuch would have been aroused by that. For Christ's sake, give me a break."

"Hurry up!" Stefan called to us.

Sam laughed nervously and whispered to me, "Just don't tell Stefan."

"All right, but you better explain Greta's comment later—"

Stefan hollered again, "Time's wasting, boys. The longer we wait, the less time you get to rest."

We ran over to what looked like a giant rolling pin. That image would have been hilarious under normal circumstances, but this particular over-sized kitchen implement was suspended between two pine trees, about forty feet in the air.

"Oh, hells no!" I shouted.

Stefan stood on a limb of one of the trees and called down to us, "Thanks for volunteering to go first, Carter."

I cursed under my breath. "Is there a ladder or something?"

Kirner came out of the barn carrying heavy ropes. That didn't look promising. He snorted and called up to Stefan, *"Denkt er, dass dies eine Yogaklasse ist?"*

Stefan whooped in response. *"Wir müssen vorsichtig mit den kindern sein."*

Sam gave Stefan the finger and yelled, "You have to be careful with the kids, do you? And no, Kirner, we don't think this is a yoga class."

"You need to teach me German," I muttered and walked toward the giant pine that supported our first obstacle. Every branch lower than fifteen feet from the ground had been sawn off. The bark had been removed too, and some sort of waxy resin had been rubbed over the surface, which made it impossible to get a grip. I walked around the base of the tree, my boots squelching in mud and dead pine needles. When I found the lowest branch, I crouched down and pushed off with the power from my legs. I reached the branch easily, but as soon as I'd wrapped my hands around it, I heard a crack. I fell onto my back in the mud with a whump. The heavy tree branch landed on my face.

"Fuck," I groaned. I sat up and checked the end of the branch. Sure enough, it had been sawn three-quarters of the way through. I turned to glare at Kirner, who grinned back and waved. I got pissed. With a loud roar, I leaped up and cleared the lower branches. The feeling was sensational and horrendously frightening at the same time. I grabbed two branches and got my feet planted into a notch of the tree. From then on, it was easy. I reached the giant roller-thing without even gasping for air.

Stefan smiled broadly. "That was great, Carter. Pretty

fucking unbelievable actually."

"Really? Why?"

"Because you looked like a fucking monkey. It only took you six seconds to climb up here."

I blinked in surprise. "Is that fast?"

"Faster than any of us," Kirner said. "I will go and bring Freyr."

"No, please don't," I said. "Let me do this on my own. Just tell me exactly what this is."

Stefan rubbed his hands together with excitement. "This is the Log of Doom. It's used to learn balance and landing technique."

"Landing technique?" I asked with a shudder.

"Yes. It's a two-for-one. You have to try and balance for as long as you can, and when you fall—and you *will* fall—you can work on landing on your feet instead of your face or other vital parts of your anatomy. Don't worry, though. Kirner's very good at setting broken bones."

"Hey, Stefan?" I asked.

"Yeah?"

"Fuck you."

He laughed and demonstrated just how fast the log would spin. Then he held it still while I shimmied across it. Once I was able to steady myself, he let go. The ground was so far away that I wanted to feel ill, but . . . I couldn't. It was so odd. My morbid fear of heights had vanished. With my sight so much sharper than any human's, I looked down at the forest floor and smiled. It was pretty.

"Hey, Carter?" Stefan said, breaking me out of my trance.

"What?" I looked over at him and was puzzled to see him staring back at me as though I had eight heads.

He raised both eyebrows and said something to Kirner in German. Kirner nodded and set off toward the house. I shrugged and began to walk slowly on the log, using it as a treadmill. I had just started jogging when Kirner returned with Freyr.

"Holy fuck," my mate said in disbelief. His expression worried me, and my balance faltered. I stopped running, but the log didn't stop moving. I felt it slip out from under my feet, but I didn't fall. Instead, I leaned sideways and planted one hand on the worn surface of the log. I kicked my legs over into a handstand, my body straight as a plank, but wobbling slightly back and forth from the effort of stopping the log from moving.

"That's just fucking weird!" someone yelled.

I lifted my head to see a small crowd gathered with Sam. It was Greta who'd spoken. She gestured wildly to Freyr, and if the blood hadn't been rushing to my head, I would've heard the conversation. I needed to get down, but didn't really want to fall so far. I closed my eyes to calm down, and an odd feeling swelled up in me. A burst of heat whipped through me, and I opened my eyes.

It was as though I was on another planet. The colors were bright like Kodachrome, and the edges of things were so sharp they appeared white. I could see the current in the air and could name a hundred different smells that assaulted my nose. I heard someone jogging along the main road, and I could tell it was a woman by the length of her stride. She also had a dog—no, two dogs, with her. I looked down and I knew that the ground was exactly forty-seven feet, eight and three quarter inches away from my hand. I knew that what I was experiencing was not normal, and I should have been scared shitless, but I harnessed the surge of power and calmed my speeding heart. The distress I felt turned into amused curiosity.

"Oh, okay," I said nonchalantly, and flipped my legs over my head.

"Carter!" Freyr screamed. "Don't just drop. *What the fuck?*"

One moment I was on the log, the next I was standing at Freyr's side, trying to figure out why everyone was backing away from me. The feeling of invincibility was gone, and I was suddenly terrified.

There was a loud thump behind me, and the ground shook a little. Stefan hurried past me to stand in front of Sam. Was he protecting his mate from me?

I whimpered and asked, "Freyr? What's wrong? Why are you all acting like that?"

Greta took her hand away from her mouth and said, "You just flew."

"Oh, ha, ha," I said dryly, but when no one else cracked a smile, I stumbled backward, until I tripped over a root and fell on my ass.

Freyr knelt down and took my hand. "She's telling the truth, Carter. You glided down from that log. And the way you were balancing . . . Have you ever taken gymnastics?"

"Never. I was always too klutzy. Will you all stop acting like this? I'm really freaking out. Is it really so rare to have a vampire who can hover and shit?"

My mate kissed me on the forehead. "You didn't hover, no. As far as gliding goes, there are some, but I have only known one other who could control their body like you did."

I scoffed. "Let me guess. Is it Alder?"

He held me at arm's length. "He was powerful, yes, but I meant Lyulf."

Chapter Fourteen—Carter

"No way!" I cried in a panic. "What is it with me and your family? If you even think about suggesting that somehow I have Lyulf's moldy-ass blood in my veins, I'm going to go insane!"

Quincy laughed. "Moldy-ass blood?"

"Seriously, Quince? You're messing with me right now?"

"Point taken."

Freyr stepped in. "It's all right, love. I'm not saying that Lyulf has come back from the . . . undead-dead and jabbed you in your sleep. I'm sure there's an explanation for this. You may just have natural talent."

I saw the doubt in his eyes, and I buried my head in my hands, sobbing. He lifted me into his arms and carried me into the house. When we were in our bedroom, he put me down on the bed and lay down behind me. I pulled his arms tight around me and shook.

He kissed my hair. "Please, love. I'm not going to tell you to calm down, because we both know this is very strange, and you have every right to be upset, but try and save your energy. That type of exertion will wear you down quickly."

I nodded and took deep breaths until the shaking stopped. I turned in Freyr's arms and took in his scent, which further relaxed my overtaxed mind. "Am I turning into Alder? Could his bond with me be growing somehow?"

"Honestly, I don't know. But—" He sat up suddenly and hit the call button on the wall near the bed. He'd had a panic alarm installed in every room, connected to the security office.

Within seconds, Stefan rushed in with Kirner and Quincy. "What is it?" the latter panted.

Freyr asked, "Did you go through all the footage from the clinic? Even after you found the nurse?"

Stefan's eyebrows drew down and he looked embarrassed. "No, we didn't. I'm sorry."

"Not your fault," Freyr replied. "Once we found her, it didn't seem necessary to keep scanning the rest of the footage."

Quincy's eyes grew wide. "Holy mother of God," he mumbled. "She was there for a month before we stopped administering the IVAS, but who knows what she was up to after that!"

"Exactly," my mate said. "None of us considered the fact she was there for weeks after that. We need to go over every frame of the feeds and figure out what she was up to."

I tried to take my mind off the latest plot twist in my life by beginning the inventory of Freyr's painting collection. It was early October, my favorite time of year, but I had no desire to be anywhere near other people—or vampires—so I lost myself in my monumental task.

Late one Friday night, Stefan came down on the pretext of bringing me something to drink. I took the mug and noted the laptop under his arm.

"What's that?"

He seemed nervous, which was completely out of character. "I thought you might like to see this. Freyr doesn't know about it, but I . . . oh, I don't know. I've always kept it separate from the other footage, and I scanned it myself to make sure that woman wasn't on it. Then I edited some of the footage together for you."

"Oh, thanks." I accepted the laptop from him, bursting with curiosity.

"Yeah. Like I said, you don't have to watch it, but I thought it might help. See you later." He turned at the door and grinned. "By the way, I didn't watch that last part."

As soon as he shut the door, I switched on the computer and curled up on the big, overstuffed sofa I'd brought in to make my work conditions a little less tomb-like. Sipping my hot chocolate, I hit *PLAY*.

"Oh my God." My jaw dropped when I saw it was the security footage from my room at the clinic. I saw myself in the hospital bed, covers up to my chest. In a bed next to me was my brother, Jacob. Whereas I merely looked asleep, Jake was hooked up to a ventilator, heart monitors, and several IV tubes.

Freyr entered the room. "Hey, guys," he said. "Sorry I'm late. That meeting was so dull! This weather doesn't help."

He leaned down to kiss my cheek. "I love you, Carter." Then he went around to Jake's side and kissed his forehead. "How're you doing today, buddy? I brought a couple new DVDs. Figured you'd be sick of those by now."

My heart swelled as I watched him talk to my brother as though he was sitting across the dinner table. I choked with emotion at the tenderness and compassion my mate showed. The theme music to some anonymous children's cartoon began playing in the background.

Freyr then said, "If you don't mind, Jake, I'm going to keep the sound down a little. I want to read to your brother."

He pulled a chair up to my bed. "Ugh, Carter. Why did you have to be in the middle of Jane Eyre? Lowner gushed over this book for months after he read it. However, I'll amuse you and keep going. At least it's getting to the good part. Okay, when last we left her, Jane was agreeing to marry that idiotic missionary."

Freyr sat back in the chair. He read for a few minutes before slowly stopped reading and let the book drop to the floor. He took my had and whispered, "Oh, Carter. Jesus, if I could take it all back I would. I would have loved you from a distance for the rest of your life if I'd known that this would be the consequence of my selfishness."

Shifting my form in the bed slightly, Freyr crawled in and curled his body against my side. Then he settled his head against my shoulder and lifted my hand to his lips. "Please, my love. Please forgive me."

His eyes closed and he slept.

Back in the present, I realized I was clutching a pillow to my chest, biting into the material to stifle my sobs. I'd never experienced anything so tender and emotional. To witness what Freyr went through in just ten minutes, then to think of what ten months of it must have been like . . . my heart hurt for him. The sadness was too much for me to take.

Then, remembering Stefan's puzzling comment about the end of the video, I clicked on the last scene. I hoped it would make me feel a little better, and it certainly did. It was from after I'd woken, the first time I fed from Freyr — the closest I'd ever get to making a sex-tape with him. I watched as our bodies rubbed together, and my cock began to swell with the memory. Freyr lifted his wrist to my mouth and said, "Take my blood, Carter." My balls tightened painfully.

"Oh, fuck!" I moaned, remembering the taste and thickness of his sweet flavor. I pinched the base of my dick hard to stop the rapidly approaching orgasm and winced in pain. Then I shut the laptop and ran upstairs to find my mate.

CHAPTER FIFTEEN—CARTER

For Columbus Day weekend, I wanted to get out of the house and do some much needed shopping. While I liked the clothes Greta had purchased for me online, I wanted to get out and get my own things.

"At least take Sam," Freyr said, not looking up from his paperwork.

I slammed my hand down onto his desk. That got his attention. With a bitter voice, I said, "At least look at me as you're patronizing me."

"I'm confused," he said slowly. "How am I patronizing you?"

"I do not believe this!" I yelled. "Perhaps by telling me I can't go out of this Goddamned house without a fucking babysitter. I have a better idea. Why not just build me a cage, and maybe a fenced-off area in the yard to run around in."

Freyr's eyebrow shot up. His calm demeanor didn't fool me. He was pissed. "Carter, I'm trying to protect you from Alder."

"But I'm a vampire now. Aren't I as strong as he is?"

"Babe, no one is as strong as Alder is. Don't you get that?"

I meekly took a chair and he exhaled slowly. "Everything I do is for a purpose. When Alder hurt you the first time, I swore I'd never let you be hurt again. Look how many times I've broken that vow." The fear and sadness in his eyes softened my anger, and I held my hand out to him. He knelt and put his head in my lap. "I won't survive if something happens to you, Carter. I don't know if I could handle it again."

I brushed the hair off his cheek and said, "But I can't live in a bubble. The longer I stay cooped up in this house, the more out of touch with reality I'll become. I need to get out. Just a small trip into town."

He kissed my fingers and asked, "Can you promise to be back by five?"

"That sounds good. I'll take the Jag."

"You'll take the Rover."

I rolled my eyes and acquiesced. "Fine."

"I need to go over a few things with you, though."

"I think I can remember. Gas pedal on the right, brake on left, use my blinkers, and look twice before pulling—"

Freyr yanked me down onto his lap. "You're such a smart-ass. Now sit up and listen. I have to tell you about how to deal with humans."

It struck me I hadn't seen a human since I'd left the clinic, and I was suddenly petrified. "Oh my God! Am I gonna attack everyone?"

"Of course not. Most humans who see you will have no idea of what you are, but there are those who pick up on subtle things—your smell, your looks, the way you walk. If those people begin to get too nosy, you need to distract them."

"How?"

"By putting thoughts into their heads."

"Huh?"

He laughed. "Look straight in the person's eyes, let your mind open to theirs, and make them hear you. Like this."

Freyr's eyes seemed to swirl blue and gray, and I heard his voice in my head. *Do you know how many naughty things I want to do to you right now?*

"That's wild!" I said.

"It's hard to describe how to do it, but you'll find it's really easy with practice. Go ahead."

I snickered. "All right. Here goes." Focusing deep into his eyes, I felt the same adrenaline rush I'd experienced on the

Log of Doom. Each individual sliver of color in his iris was vivid and distinct, and I could see how the flutter of his eyelashes tickled the air. His pupils dilated as I blazed my gaze into his mind. I began to describe exactly what I wanted him to do to me, but I stopped when his heart rate suddenly went through the roof. His throat began to spasm as he struggled for air, and he fell to the floor. Once his eyes rolled back into his head, he went into a full-blown seizure.

"Stefan!" I screamed. "Help me!"

A crowd of people came running, with Stefan in the lead. He knelt next to Freyr's shaking form. "What the hell happened?"

"I don't know," I sobbed. "He was teaching me how to put my thoughts into someone's head, and when I tried it on him, he started acting like this."

He shook his head in frustration. "You did this to him just by projecting your thoughts?"

I nodded frantically and backed away. "I didn't mean to hurt him."

Stefan said, "He's in shock, and he needs blood. Carter, come here."

"No," I said. "Not after I hurt him."

"Fuck this," he said and bit into his own wrist. Freyr latched on and sucked hard on the offering.

Watching him feed my mate was one of the most desolate moments of my life. Greta tried to put an arm around me, but I shook her off. "Don't touch me," I hissed. "There's something wrong with me."

Sam stepped toward me. "Carter, he's fine."

"Leave me alone!"

I jumped out of the window, crossed the lawn, and easily cleared the boundary wall. I slowed to a walk when I reached the edge of a country club in Westchester, since a man running faster than a cheetah through a golf course might draw unwelcome attention. Part of me wanted to go home and beg Freyr to forgive me for hurting him as I had. But no—I couldn't go back. They weren't safe around me. I was a freak. I was *ab*normal among *para*normals. How twisted was that?

A jogging trail lay just off the main road, along the outside of the course. I listened to the *thwump-tick* of clubs striking balls. On the links, men discussed business transactions and their new secretaries. In the clubhouse, women gossiped about fashion and the hot new caddy with the British accent. My nose stung with the tang of freshly mown grass, cologne, and booze.

I wished to God my senses would dull down a little so I could think. But my nose suddenly picked up on something that brought me to a halt. Although I didn't recognize the source, I could smell blood nearby.

After the stress of the day, I was thirsty, and the temptation was too great. Turning back the way I'd come, I followed the savory-sweet scent until I heard a wail of anguish. The hairs on my neck stood on end. Fifty yards ahead, in a small clearing, I saw a young woman sprawled on the ground, blood pooled around her. At first, I would've said that an animal had attacked her—the wound in her throat was ragged and sloppy. Then another smell drifted close, and I crouched into a defensive position.

"Who the hell's out there?" I growled to the other vampire who was approaching me.

"Now is that any way to treat an old friend?" The voice froze my heart, and I couldn't move. He came out into the clearing, and I knew that he was no stranger at all.

"Alder," I whispered.

He hadn't changed at all. Impeccably dressed in a perfectly-fitted gray suit, he looked ridiculously out of place amidst the scene of carnage.

He smiled a serpent's grin. "Hello, pet."

"Don't call me that," I said, backing slowly away.

"Now why not? Certainly I can call my mate whatever I like."

I wanted to vomit. "You're delusional."

"I don't think so. What is amazing to me is that Secundus hasn't figured it out yet." He began laughing in that smooth tenor voice that could bring any man or woman to their knees. With all my strength, I fought the urge to do just that.

"He's figured out everything," I lied, trying to sound confident.

"If my brother had figured out everything, he certainly wouldn't have let you out of his sight. I'm glad he did, though. Saved me a lot of trouble. Now I don't have to carry out my big attack on the compound, because you just fell right into my lap. Your timing couldn't have been more perfect."

Anger danced in my eyes. "Your *heart* will be in your lap if you try to come near me."

Alder put a hand to his heart in mock astonishment. "Why, Carter! Could it be you've grown a spine?"

"Fuck you."

"Later, definitely. Right now, we have to get going."

I laughed. "Who's *we?* What makes you think I'd go with you?"

He yawned and said, "My sweet pet, what makes you think you have a choice?"

Four shapes rushed out of the woods around me, and I was on the ground before I could blink. I thrashed and kicked and sent one of my attackers flying into a tree. Alder got down on his haunches and said, "Wow. My pet is all grown up. Tell me, though. Did Stefan teach you how to defend yourself against a dagger to the lungs?"

The question was so unexpected that I said simply, "What?"

"Hmph, apparently not. His loss."

Too quickly for me, a dagger was in his hand and thrust into my chest. The jewel-encrusted hilt ripped the cloth of my shirt, and I grunted in pain. Drawing breath was impossible, so I lay there on my side in exquisite agony, blood drenching the dead leaves under me. I grabbed at Alder's arm, but my fingers weren't strong enough to hold. My arm fell like a slack rope.

"Oh, don't worry, pet. I just can't have you struggling during the trip. Once we're in the plane, I'll get you a snack. You'll be fine."

Plane. Trip. Snack. Fine . . .

No. Not fine. I coughed up a mouthful of blood and mumbled, "Why are you doing this?"

He stood up and brushed dirt off his black pants. "Because, pet. You were the one that got away. And nothing — *nothing* — ever gets away from me."

My pulse faded, and I fell into blackness.

The low buzz of a jet engine woke me. Immediately I felt for the dagger, but it had been removed. I was lying on a bed, in nothing but my boxers.

"Good evening," said a female voice.

I recognized her at once. "You were at the hospital, then in my room."

"Right on both counts. I'm Caroline."

Two guards hauled me into a chair and left the room. A scantily clad young woman straddled my lap and leaned in to sniff my throat. She purred, and I grimaced.

"You do realize I'm gay, right?" I said, twitching as she ran talon-like nails down my arms.

She took a long strand of her wavy chestnut hair and tickled my face with it. I slapped her hand away, and she pretended to be hurt. "Ouch," she whined.

"Listen, bitch. Don't try it. I'm immune to you."

"You say that now . . ." she purred, squeezing my nipples gently.

My brows drew down, and I tilted my head in thought. "Um . . . No, I'll always say that. In fact, I'd rather fuck a meat grinder."

The little vixen was persistent. Her hips ground down on mine, and she pulled off her shirt to reveal an enormous bosom overflowing a lacy, scarlet bra. She bit her lip seductively and said, "What do you think?"

"I think I have curtains that color."

That did it. Her expression changed from cute and innocent to evil and angry. She shrieked and punched me in the face. "You little shit. If you want to make it hard on yourself, then I have a question for you."

I gave her a cheeky grin. "Yes, your ass does look fat in those pants."

She slapped me that time, but quickly regained her composure. "What I was *going* to ask is, are you thirsty, Carter? Bring them in."

The door opened, and my eyes widened in horror. The guards tossed two humans into the room and then backed out. Caroline picked one up by the throat and held him at arm's length. "This one is Thomas, and that other one is Cory. Alder has been toying with them for a while, just for you. Take a look." She threw the poor kid onto the bed and ripped the clothes off his quivering body. A rigid erection bobbed as he gasped for air and moaned.

"Please," he begged. "Yes, take me. Oh, fuck!"

Caroline kissed him and bit his lower lip. The boy laughed through his nose and tilted his hips up against her. She then knelt by the other kid and stripped him. Again, he was on the brink of orgasm. God only knew how long Alder had been teasing them.

She smiled sweetly at me. "Here's your dinner. If you don't

finish them, I will, and it won't be pretty or quick."

The door slammed behind her when she left, and I was alone with the grisly offering. I panicked. I'd never had human blood before, and I didn't know what would happen. The boy Caroline had called Cory said, "Please, kill us. They tortured our friends. Please. Do what you have to do, just have mercy."

I took a deep breath and said, "O-okay. I'll try to be gentle."

Thomas barked out a laugh. "Don't be gentle. I want to go with a fucking smile on my face." He gripped my shoulders and hauled my body onto his. Then he offered his throat, and said, "Thank you."

Had it not been for those words, I could never have sunk my fangs into his throat. He bucked and rubbed himself against me as I drank his blood, and I was grateful that I wasn't in the least aroused by the situation.

The difference between vampire and human blood was incredible. Even though it didn't taste nearly as good as Freyr's, it was as though I'd just been introduced to espresso after a steady diet of decaf. I grunted with satisfaction, and sucked at the wound until the young man's heart stopped beating.

Cory stared at Thomas' glazed eyes and shook in terror. I moved the body from the bed and then turned to frightened man.

"It'll be quick," I promised. "I can snap your neck if you'd rather —"

"No. Take what you need." He smiled weakly.

After he was gone, I pulled on my clothes that were folded in a chair next to the bed. Then I opened the bedroom door and walked into the main cabin. Alder was reading *Great Expectations* and didn't acknowledge my presence. Caroline was in the corner, giving a fully-clothed lap dance to a well-dressed man. They were whispering about mates and love, so I assumed they were attached.

More power to him.

It was as though I was invisible until we finally touched down in Munich. Alder smiled at me. "If you try anything, it won't be pretty. Don't forget what I can do."

Lucifer himself could not have sneered as perfectly as Alder did then. From a briefcase at his feet, he produced a teddy bear—a small, tan bear streaked with dried blood. Jacob's bear. Rage burned in my eyes. I could feel the heat rush through my veins, and my senses sharpened. My new-found beast was struggling to take over, but even with my ridiculously quick reflexes and incredible powers, there was no way I could accomplish anything onboard a plane. I had to wait to get him alone before I pulled that ace out of my sleeve. I calmed down and glared at the vampire, inwardly reveling in the fact he had no idea what was in store for him.

After we'd landed, taxied into a private hangar and climbed down from the plane, I put my plan into action. While Alder dealt with the customs agents, I locked my gaze with a pretty blonde who was checking our forged passports. Mine must have been forged, but she didn't seem to notice anything. When she looked at me, I smiled and unleashed my beast, hoping to hell I wasn't going to kill her where she stood. Her eyes glazed over and I knew I'd captured her interest.

I thought, *Don't look at me. Just scratch your arm if you understand me.*

She nonchalantly reached up and ran her nails across the sleeve of her uniform. I continued, *Good girl. Call this number: 733-555-6902. It's in the U.S. Ask for Freyr and tell him that Alder has taken Carter to Munich. Will you do that for me, beautiful? Just bite your lip if you will.*

Straight white teeth caught her plump lip, and my heart soared. Alder didn't have a clue he was about to have his ass kicked from here to kingdom come.

Chapter Sixteen—Freyr

As soon as I came to and realized Carter was missing, I went nuts. They'd found a small pool of his blood in the woods near the house and detected the scent of several vampires. There were traces of a struggle too. My mate had been taken. I sent out every member of the guard in different directions and had the house staff call every watcher on the planet they could find. I sat on our bed, huddled with Titus. He whimpered, and I kissed his head.

"Daddy's all right. He'll come back soon." I put Titus down on the end of the bed, but he crawled back up and lay on Carter's pillow. I almost moved him, but I indulged him just this once. I dragged myself from bed and moved like a zombie toward the kitchen, but I was intercepted by Stefan on my way.

"We have something!" he said with excitement. He practically dragged me to the security office, where we joined everyone else in the house who'd come to hear the news. Stefan nodded to an IT technician named Michael to report his findings.

He cleared his throat nervously. "I reviewed all the footage that our subject appeared in, and I noticed this." After a few keystrokes, video came up on the large wall monitor. It was the phony nurse, standing in the medication storage room where Carter's IVAS had been kept. Michael played the footage in slow motion and continued, "Here she's removing what looks to be a unit of IVAS from her purse and she places it in the refrigeration case."

"She brought it in?" I asked incredulously. "Were they fake or something?"

"That's what I wondered. So last night, I went to cryogenics storage and took small samples from the labels of every unit of Mr. Denwright's IVAS supply that was left and compared them with an authentic IVAS label from our facility. I discovered that seven out of twenty units in Mr. Denwright's supply were counterfeit."

"Good God!" Lowner cried. "That's brilliant, Michael."

"But where does that leave us?" I asked.

"Well, sir," the nervous tech said, "I took the liberty of testing the DNA of the counterfeit units against the known sample from Mr. Denwright."

"Was it mixed with something?" Stefan asked.

"No, sir. There was no trace of Mr. Denwright's blood in the counterfeit units. It all belonged to one man who is a close relative of Mr. Amsel."

"Alder," I hissed. "He'd been pumping Carter full of his blood. What purpose would that serve?"

Sam asked, "Michael, how many counterfeit units did you say were left?"

"Seven," was the answer. "And I found a total of nineteen instances on camera where the subject brought units in with her."

"So it's possible Carter was given at least twelve units," Sam said. "Enough to make his body think it had been mated to Alder."

"What?" I roared. "Are you trying to tell me now Carter isn't even my real mate?"

I threw a chair across the room and it splintered against the wall. Lowner took me by the shoulders and shook me hard. "Of course he's your mate. You know as well as anyone that blood bonding is only secondary to what's in your heart. Alder is just trying to get at you."

"It's fucking working!"

Greta, who had been uncharacteristically silent, suddenly hopped up and said, "Oh holy crap! I think I know what's going on with Carter's rare abilities."

"I'm open to any ideas," Stefan replied.

She ran shaking fingers through her hair and said, "When we mate, our blood is physically bonded to our partner's, correct?"

"Yes."

"Okay, with humans, both parents' blood types are the factors in their children's blood types. So let's say that Carter's and Alder's blood formed A positive. And when Freyr's blood—let's call it B negative—was transplanted into his system, Carter's body couldn't fight it."

"*And*," I prodded her.

She continued, "What would happen if maybe—just maybe—Carter's body synthesized it instead of fighting it? Maybe the A positive cells allowed the B negative cells to bond."

"Three vamps' blood bonding?" Quincy said. "Impossible."

"How do you know that?" Greta asked. "Just because we've never seen it doesn't mean it hasn't happened. Think about it. It explains so much."

Sam nodded. "It's possible that it magnified the effect of a normal bonding. If Carter's blood is now growing with two bonds from two of the most powerful and ancient vampires in the world, the result would be . . ."

Quincy whistled and said, "Super Vamp."

Those words soaked through the haze and made perfect sense. "Good lord," I said. "We have to find him before he accidentally . . . so we can help him control his power."

"If only we could find him," Sam said sadly.

A shrill ringtone brought me back to earth. I pulled my

phone from my pocket and answered it.

"Hallo, this is Freyr?" a female said. I noticed a strong German accent.

"Yes," I said cautiously.

She sounded relieved. "Yes, sir. I am Pia Jonson. I work in a private hangar at the airport here in Munich, Germany. And I may be crazy, but a man spoke in my head and—"

"You're not crazy," I said. "Please tell us exactly what happened."

"*Ja*, okay. This man who spoke in my mind said to call you and tell you that Alder has taken Carter to Munich."

Terror and rage made my blood boil, and my fangs lengthened. I could barely ask her, "Did Carter seem injured in any way?"

"No, he was not hurt. But I do not think they are staying in the city, sir."

Stefan asked, "Why do you think that?"

"Because I heard the other men talking about the trip to a castle."

"Drubich," I said with a sigh. "Thank you, *Fräulein*."

I ended the call. Sam said, "If Carter could control himself enough to project into that woman's thoughts, then I think Alder has made a big mistake."

"What mistake?" I replied.

He looked at me and smiled. "Carter's smart. He'll bide his time until the moment's right to strike. He's a lethal weapon, and Alder's too arrogant and stupid to even think it would be possible for Carter to be stronger than him. In other words, your brother has no idea he's just brought the proverbial Trojan horse right through his own front door."

CHAPTER SEVENTEEN—CARTER

I'd always imagined Drubich Castle as a sprawling palace of gleaming white stone, with high turrets and crenellated walls, geometrically designed gardens, and a moat running quietly around the base of the battlements. I pictured it situated in a wide, green valley, where a warm wind shifted the grass like a billowing sheet.

As the castle came into view, however, I realized I had laboring under a serious misapprehension. My imagined lush valley was in truth a high, rugged peak, with the castle balanced on a small plateau halfway up the desolate mountainside. The area immediately surrounding the structure was devoid of trees, but the forests along the roads were thick with larch. Their needles had fallen, making them look like claws rising up from the ground, as though Alder had some evil army buried in his backyard. A fierce, bitter gale made the bare branches creak and scrape together.

When I got a closer look at Freyr's ancestral home, I was further disillusioned. In place of a gently flowing moat, a rushing brook swept under a wooden bridge and along one wall of the castle. The spray of water had covered the face of the stone with a greenish slime, and moss had taken hold.

The caravan of SUVs came to a stop just before the bridge, and the driver of the lead vehicle got out to open a newly constructed metal gate. I snorted. "Seriously, you have a gate? Who the hell are you trying to keep out? *Frankenberry* and *Count Chocula?*"

He didn't rise to the bait, so I tried again. When we finally

139

reached the portcullis, I inhaled deeply and said, "Ah! Home crap home."

Alder's jaw clenched as though he was grinding his teeth, and I mentally congratulated myself. At least I knew I could get to him. However, I figured it'd be smart to get to the guards first. The customs agent at the airport seemed to respond to me, so maybe I could brainwash Alder's evil troops. But how could I do it without looking right at them? That would be a little obvious. I stared at the back of the guard in front of me, concentrating on his heartbeat and his even breathing. I let the heat flood through me and—

"Ah!" the guard cried. He clutched his head and doubled over in the passenger seat. I let go of my thought, and he straightened.

"What's the matter with you, Clement?" Alder asked.

The vamp shook his head quickly to clear the confusion. "I'm sorry, sir. A sudden headache." I tapped into him again and he grunted. "Damn!"

I bit my lip to keep from laughing. Well, at least I knew I could migraine them to into submission. Of course, I might send them into convulsions and nearly kill them, as I had my mate. That was why I was in this mess in the first place. I'd hurt him, and instead of facing the problem, I ran away like a little child. Now I'd put us all in danger. If Freyr and the others came to get me, there was a high probability that one of my friends might be hurt . . . or worse. I put my head in my hands and tried not to sob. Unfortunately, a small choke escaped me.

"Aww," Alder cooed. "Feeling homesick?"

With no energy left in my voice, I replied, "What do you want from me? Do you honestly think I'll just sit here and play happy family?"

"What fun would that be? If you'll remember, I like it rough."

Even though I knew I'd never submit to him in that way, the memories of Alder raping me made me nauseous. The weeks and months I spent at his mercy took all of the fight out of me for a moment. Then Freyr's face came into my mind, and I focused on his gorgeous image. I thought of his lop-sided grin as he teased my body, and his hungry grunts as he took my blood. I refused to give that up. I wasn't going down without a fight.

I turned to Alder. "Yes, I remember. What you lacked in size and technique, you made up for in enthusiasm." I didn't think he'd punch me, but he did, and my head hit the window hard enough to smash it. I looked at the spider-web cracks, and asked, "Now how will you explain that to the insurance company? *Well, you see my prisoner smart-mouthed me about my non-existent dick and I slammed his –* " My head went completely through the window that time. I brushed pieces of glass out of my hair and groaned. "Fuck me, that hurt! That's not an invitation, by the way."

"Shut up!" he screamed. "I'll break your fucking neck if you don't shut up!"

"Say *please*," I said with a smile.

He reached over and opened my door, then shoved me onto the ground. When I stood up, I did shut up. Not to make Alder happy, but because of what I saw. All around us, vampires were hard at work, mending the crumbling stonework, laying pipes and wires, and even planting shrubbery. The interior courtyard of the castle was so vastly different from the exterior that my jaw dropped, and I looked around, speechless.

Alder snickered. "Thank God! I thought you'd never stop talking. I was getting a headache."

Despite my interest in the surroundings, his patronizing tone pissed me off. *I'll give you a fucking headache.* I tapped into Clement's head again. I heard him gasp, and I smiled to myself. I let go quickly and he staggered toward a door, holding his head.

"What's wrong with him?" another one of the guards asked.

"Go find out, Hans," Alder ordered.

The man bowed slightly, and I half expected him to click his heels together and salute, but I didn't want to irritate the *Führer* right then. I wanted answers.

"What is this place?" I asked.

"Finally, a sensible question," Alder replied with a laugh. "This is the inner ward, the courtyard around the palace. What I'm doing now are some badly needed restorations before this place falls to the ground."

"But why save the castle at all? What's the point?"

He smiled graciously. "I want to create a place of higher learning—a university of sorts, in which to study the history and culture of the vampire race."

I stared at him for a long time, not quite believing what he'd said. When it finally filtered through my head, I doubled over and cackled. "You really have gone insane, haven't you? The Alder von Drubich Center for Bloodlust and Gore. Holy shit, that's funny! I can see the course list now. Bloodsuckers 101, Psychology of the Dead, and . . . ooh! I have a perfect idea. Myths and Folklore: Was Vlad the Impaler Really A Vampire, Or Was He Just A Crazy Bastard?"

"Something like that, yes." His straight-faced answer was not what I expected. I opened my mouth to speak, but then shut it and shook my head.

A tall redhead with pouty Botox'ed lips hurried toward us. She surprised me by wrapping her arms around Alder and plastering her mouth to his. While he didn't seem as happy to see her as she was to see him, he did return the embrace and kiss her back. At first, I was inexplicably jealous. Then I realized this bitch might just keep Psycho off my ass—literally.

Not that he was going to be anywhere near me anyway, but there were definite advantages to being cuckolded. Still, the display confused me.

When the two pried away from each other, I cleared my throat and asked, "Should I be worried, darling?"

The woman chuckled and sneered at me. "Who are you?"

I shrugged. "He told me I was his mate, but apparently it's an open relationship."

"*Mate?*" she cried. "But Alder —"

He didn't acknowledge her outburst. "Carter, this is my decorator, Dahlia."

"Decorator?" she screamed. I heard by her accent that was American. She balled her fists and glared. "You son of a bitch. *That's* what you were doing all this time?"

Alder's eyes flashed red, and his voice was like a smoldering fire. He gripped her elbow and growled. "What I do is *my* business. Don't you ever speak to me like that again, or I will destroy you. Do you understand me?"

Everyone stopped and watched the confrontation. From their reactions, I guessed it wasn't the first time Alder had shown his true nature. Dahlia's lip trembled, and she begged, "I'm sorry. Please, let me go."

He threw her to the ground and walked away. I put a hand out to help her up, but she shied back, so I left her there in the dirt and followed Alder inside.

It was a surreal experience, walking into the great hall. I remembered Freyr's diary, and his account of the horrifying things that happened in this room when Lyulf and the others. I paused in the doorway, and Alder turned to me. "What are you waiting for? Do you want to be carried over the threshold?"

Without answering him, I stepped into the room and went back five centuries in time. The lower sections of the walls were paneled with dark wood. Above the panelling was light gray stone, stained over the years by soot from candles and the huge fireplace at the far end of the room. It reminded me a lot of Freyr's home, but whereas the latter was filled with light from large windows, this hall was forbidding and dark. The stone seemed to suck the light out of the air. The only windows were high up on the walls.

A tall, lanky man entered through the far door and walked toward me, holding his hand out and smiling like an idiot. He said, "*Willkommen, Herr Denwright. Ich heisse Klaus. Wenn Sie etwas brauchen, bitte nachfragen.*"

I rolled my eyes and sighed dramatically. "Blah, blah, blah, achten shingen dingaling." I looked at Alder and asked, "All right, Adolf. What'd he say?"

Alder growled quietly. "For Christ's sake! The first thing you are doing is starting German lessons."

"Excellent," I said with mock excitement. "What's the German for *Is that your penis? I thought it was a toothpick.*"

His hand wrapped around my throat, smashed my head into the stone wall, then hissed in my ear, "Listen, you bastard. I'm not going to be very happy with you if you don't stop all of this right now."

I could have leaned forward right then and ripped his throat out, but I controlled the insane urge. I had to find out what was really going on in that castle. I wasn't buying the Drubich County Community College explanation. I nodded my acquiescence, and Alder let me go.

Along one wall were several display cases housing artifacts from Freyr's family history. It was macabre. In a shadow box frame on the wall were a bow and several arrows. The card on the wall described the items.

Bow and Arrows, German, 1425-1450
Used in the execution of the vampires, Lyulf von Drubich and his wife Ershabet, April 1457.
Gift of Mr. Alder Eberly

"Still using a fake last name?" I muttered to myself. "What a douche."

Alder snuck up behind me. "Look at this."

In the next display case was a long sword, held up with brass mounts. Without seeing the card, I knew what it was, but I still read it because I couldn't quite believe Alder would display such items with pride.

Sword, French, c. 1400
Used in the execution of the vampires, Lyulf von Drubich and his wife Ershabet, April 1457.
Gift of Mr. Alder Eberly

"What do you think?" Alder asked with a grin. "Too much?"

"I think you're disgusting. Those weapons killed your brothers and sister-in-law. Don't you care?"

"Not particularly. In fact, I'll let you in on a little secret." I raised an eyebrow, waiting for his big revelation. He said, "I'm the one who supplied the church with all of the information about Lyulf."

I was thunderstruck. "*You?* You handed them over to the Prince to be slaughtered? For Christ's sake, why? They were your family."

"*Wrong!*" Alder roared. "Wrong, wrong, wrong!"

"They . . . weren't your family?"

"Of course not," he said with a tired sigh. "Secundus and I are full-blooded brothers, yes, but we weren't related to Lyulf."

My head spun. "I am so confused. Why didn't Freyr tell me any of this?"

"Because he doesn't know that, my little buttercup." He grabbed my chin and tried to kiss my forehead but I twisted away. He grinned. "Freyr — as you insist on calling him — and

I were the sons of a wealthy land owner near Marburg, in Hessen. Lyulf and Ershabet came into our town one night and threatened to attack my family's home. Lyulf made a treaty that said my father could keep his land and no harm would come to his tenants if my brother and I joined the vampires."

"Why would he want you two?"

"Secundus and I were taken so my father's bloodline would end. That way, Lyulf could come and claim the land after our parents had died. We were taken and turned, and I was fine with it, but Secundus had a hard time dealing with such a shock. His memory was affected somehow, so when Lyulf told him he was his brother, Secundus accepted it without question."

"Can I ask when that was?"

"Curiosity killed the cat, you know?" he said with a playful grin.

"Well, I'm immortal, so it doesn't matter."

"Touché. The year was 1223. I was twenty-four, preparing to go get a wife somewhere, and Secundus was around twenty-two, I think. He wanted to go into the clergy."

"No way," I breathed.

Alder laughed. "Kidding. That twit didn't know what he wanted."

"But why did you kill Lyulf, if you didn't mind being turned by him?"

"When our father died and I saw the fortunes that Lyulf raked in from my family's estate, I told him I wanted the money so I could start my own clan. I couldn't stand being under his command anymore. He refused.

"Secundus puts Lyulf high on a pedestal, but he was really a brutal, selfish monster. His four brothers were the same way. So I decided to rid myself of my problems. I sent word to the priests that vampires lived in Drubich. Then I took Secundus out on a little spree one night and wiped out an entire town. You should have seen him, wrenching babies from their mothers' arms."

Revulsion made my head swim. I didn't believe him—couldn't believe him. I was so horrified at the thought of Freyr killing an innocent child I wanted to vomit. Alder saw my distress and added fire to the flames. "Secundus has always been gay, you know. That night, his bloodlust completely took over. He was finally able to sate his lust for men. There were lots of cute young men for the taking in that town, and boy did Secundus take!"

"I don't believe you," I whimpered.

"Believe it. You should be glad he killed them when he was done. Anyway, I'd written to the church before Secundus and I went on our rampage. The deal was the priests could have the glory of handing the heads of the vampires over to the church, but I would keep possession of the castle and the majority of our wealth."

"You took Freyr, though. You could've left him."

Alder's jaw clenched. "Unfortunately not, for two reasons. First, I needed him with me when we went to reclaim our father's land. Second, because Secundus' little army of friends had already escaped, I couldn't very well stroll into the woods without my brother. If the rest of them found out what I'd done, I would have been ripped into pieces, so I took Secundus and went to Switzerland. No one was any the wiser."

"So all those years, the church knew about you?"

"No. The elders of the local church who'd been part of the execution knew of my existence, but they were bound to secrecy. Actually they were in fear of their lives—I made sure of that. When they died, the secret died with them."

All I could manage to say was, "Oh."

Alder put a hand on my hip and smiled sinfully. "Now that we've completed our trip down memory lane, let's go see the bedroom."

I leaped back and growled. "I am not going to sleep in the same room as you."

"Don't get all upset," he groaned. "I've arranged another room for you, at least for tonight. You might as well make yourself at home here, pet."

"I won't be staying," I said. "Don't you think Freyr will figure out where I've gone?"

On his way up a long, steep staircase, he said, "Even if Secundus did know you are here, he doesn't have the manpower to even get inside these walls. He's always been weak."

Alder lead me to a tomb-like bedchamber on the second floor. There were some clothes on the bed, including a dinner jacket and pants.

"Why the jacket?" I asked.

He rolled his eyes. "What *has* Secundus been teaching you? In my house, you will dress for dinner, which is at seven. Until then, you stay here."

I was skeptical. "When you say "dinner," do you mean *dinner* dinner or a plasma shake?"

He didn't answer my question before slamming the door. It was the first time I'd been alone since I'd been taken by Alder. Once he was out of earshot, I finally broke down. Exhaustion made my bones ache, and my stomach heaved. I dropped onto the bed and bawled. "Freyr, please come and get me. Please. I can't do this on my own."

My heart hurt, and I wanted to give up, but I got hold of my senses. For some reason, I'd been given this extra strength. I knew I needed to learn how to control it, and quickly. I listened for Clement. He was in the kitchen, two stories below me. With just a little push, I heard him shout in pain. I realized that with a little more practice, I could bring down Alder's defenses so quickly he wouldn't know what was happening. There was no doubt Freyr would come for me. Yes, the prodigal son would soon return, and I was the key to the gate.

CHAPTER EIGHTEEN—CARTER

At ten past seven, I put on the suit, like an obedient schoolboy, and knocked on the door. A big, brawny vamp with beady eyes and a Slavic accent told me to follow him. He led me to the dining room, and when I saw the table, I laughed. A long trestle table was covered with pewter plates and huge cloth napkins, and knives and forks with ivory handles. Two benches ran along the sides of the table, which was at least twenty feet long. Alder sat at one end, naturally, and all of his nameless minions—as well as Caroline, Klaus, and Dahlia—sat on the benches. They all stopped talking when I came in.

"Pardon," I said, trying to hide my laugh. "This is the epitome of understated elegance, I gotta hand it to you, Alder."

"Sit," he commanded.

I sat down and tied the large napkin around my neck. "Cool! I feel like Henry VIII. What's for dinner? Mutton? Wild boar? Can you shove an apple in its mouth?"

One of the guards snorted, but I didn't see which. Alder didn't either, so he glared at all of them. My tease had thrown him, though, and that was my main objective—to take away his authority, a little bit at a time.

Time to push a little harder. I put my chin in my hand and started humming show tunes—quietly at first, then gradually rising in volume. I was about to start selections from *Fiddler on the Roof* when Alder smashed his hand down on the table.

"Don't you fucking dare!" Alder boomed.

Several of the guards busted up, laughing, and Alder ordered everyone out. Then he jumped over the table towards me and sent me sprawling onto the floor. I marveled at how he seemed to fly the length of the room. I knew then where I'd gotten my ability to jump so far. I was busy watching his movements, so he was on me before I could get my bearings. Fangs sank into my shoulder, and I roared. He grunted with pleasure and sucked hard.

"Get off me!" I pushed at him, but couldn't fight his hold.

"I hear the doubt in your voice," Alder whispered. "I *am* your mate. You know it. Your body knows it. You *will* forget him, and love me."

He grabbed my wrist and dragged me to the bedroom. I grabbed onto the door jamb, but couldn't hold it long. Alder pushed me onto the bed. "I love it so much when you struggle."

"Try this for struggling," I growled. I locked my knees together and kicked out with my feet. Alder rocketed into the far wall. I pounced on him and pulled him up. Squeezing with one hand, I held him at arm's length and roared. "I'm not your pet, you psycho! Freyr is my true mate. I'll always remember him!"

In my anger, I didn't hear the door open behind me. There was a small pinch, then an intense cold rush, followed by a slow burn throughout my body. I turned to see Caroline behind me, holding a large syringe in her hand. It was empty. They were doping me.

"Oh, shit," I muttered. Everything went dark.

When I came to, I kept my eyes shut and listened.

"Why is he so strong?" someone asked.

"How the fuck should I know?" Alder snapped. "How much of his blood do we have?"

"Enough for a few months."

Clement spoke then. "Can I ask, sir, why you are so obsessed with having Carter Denwright? You could have any man."

I heard high heels click across the floor. "Or any woman. I could give you what you need."

"You're getting tiresome, Dahlia. I *have* never, and *will* never want you. For a quick fuck, yes, but—"

"But nothing," she insisted. "I've given so many—no, no! Please! No!" The plea stopped with the crunch of bone and a thud. Alder said, "That's quite nasty. Get her out of here before the carpet's ruined."

The strong scent of fresh blood cleared my head even more, and it was a struggle to keep from licking my lips. I couldn't let them know I was awake. Apparently my strong system was metabolizing my IVAS in record time.

Alder answered Clement's question. "I want Carter because he's beautiful. He was the most beautiful pet I'd ever had. I want him because he fights back. He's not some idiotic twink like the ones I pick up in bars and drain the same night. I want him because my blood wants to bond with his."

"So, you feel he's your mate?"

"He *is* my mate!" Alder barked. "But Secundus stole his heart from me. Carter betrayed me, so I punished him. I never thought he would be man enough to kill himself. After he cut his throat, I thought he was dead, so I just left. I had no idea that bastard Stefan was so close by. Doesn't matter now, though. Carter's mine."

Caroline sighed. "Secundus will come for him."

"Let him. If they do make it through those walls, I can squash him like a bug. He's too weak to take me on. He always has been. His whole little gang put together could never match my power."

I smiled inwardly. *But I can, asshole.*

They left me in my room in what they thought was a drug-induced coma. I immediately began planning how to get Freyr into the castle. There had to be some chink in the armor

I could take advantage of. And, after that, I hoped that Freyr would know my heart well enough to think the same way.

Alder left the room and I heard someone approach my bed. Cold fingers reached out and grasped my cock through my pants. I knew who it was without even looking.

"Get your hand off of my dick, Caroline," I grumbled. "Or I'll snap your fingers off."

"Aw! Look who's grumpy when he wakes up."

I smacked her hand and winced at the stiffness in my neck from pretending to be unconscious. Her sneer was too much. I shot right back at her, "Aw! Look at who opens her legs to everyone and his Aunt Lillian."

She glared at me. "You'd better watch it. Barney already doesn't like you."

"Who?" I asked.

"My mate."

I snorted. "You're fucking a big, purple dinosaur?" She hauled me up and punched my jaw hard. Then she rammed a syringe into my arm. "Ow! I'm going to tell Alder you did that."

I did my best Gloria Swanson-esque swoon onto the bed and laughed when Caroline slammed the door. Then I stopped and listened very carefully.

"We're going out hunting," she said to someone outside the door.

"He told you not to leave when he's in Munich."

"Oh, come on. We'll be back before he gets home tonight."

"But—"

"For God's sake, Klaus. You're not my keeper, so fuck you. Have fun babysitting. I've given him enough blood to keep him out until Alder gets back. He said he wanted to have some fun with his mate tonight."

Oh, hell no! I had to escape, but how? Frantically, I thought about anything Freyr had ever told me about the castle, hoping for some clue as to my next move. I remembered him talking about the gates, the courtyard, the hall, the towers, the tunnel —

The tunnel. There's the hidden door behind the tapestry in the great hall. Time to explore, Denwright.

I waited until I heard Klaus walk away. I couldn't hear anyone on the second floor, where I was, so I crept to the door and tested the knob. It was unlocked. Probably a good idea, actually, since I could have just torn the door from its hinges if I really wanted to leave. The ancient iron bars bricked into my windows, however, would be practically impossible for me to remove, especially given my time constraints. It was getting dark, and Caroline had said Alder would return in the evening.

It was easy to find the library by the faint scent of musty books. I snuck in the door and searched the desk, and found a pen. I was going to take paper, but it rustled too much, so I'd have to find something else to write on. I stopped again to listen for hearts and voices. Everyone was still down in the kitchens, watching TV, so I made my move.

In the great hall, there were four tapestries, one on each wall. I supposed them to be recreations of the originals that had hung there so many centuries before. I figured out quickly, though, that the entrance to the tunnel had to be on the wall opposite the main door, since Alder and Freyr had watched the priests as they spoke. I lifted the edge of the tapestry and stared at nothing but wood paneling and stone. I cursed under my breath. They'd most likely closed the secret tunnel off during renovations.

I leaned my forehead against the wall in frustration, and happened to notice several very old gouges in the stone floor that disappeared under the paneling. Had I found it? I pushed on the panel, but nothing happened. I pushed harder. Still nothing.

"Fuck," I muttered. I was ready to give up and go back to

the room before I was caught. Then I noticed the finish on one section of molding at the top of the panel was slightly duller than the others. Could it be as simple as a wooden bar in brackets?

I carefully pushed up on the molding, and it came free with a loud click. I froze, waiting for the sound of feet to come rushing toward my hiding spot, but they didn't even mute the TV to listen. The door wasn't easy to get open, and then it suddenly gave way.

The noise was like a banshee, and two guards ran into the room. I could tell by the scent that one of them was Clement. I lit into him again with my mind, and he grunted in pain.

"Clement, maybe it's a tumor," the other guard said. I sank my fangs into my fist to stop from laughing.

"You idiot! Vampires don't get tumors. Come on, I'm tired."

"And you may have a tumor."

I heard a fist hit flesh and I winced. The guards retreated, so I fit my body through the secret door. Freyr had described taking up floorboards, so I lifted them carefully and sure enough found a rope ladder . . . a five hundred and fifty-year-old rope ladder. I yanked and pulled every which way, but it held. Before I climbed down, I remembered the stone that Alder had pulled free from the wall so he could watch what had happened that horrible night. Even with my enhanced vision, it was nearly impossible to figure out which one was loose.

Think, Denwright. Okay, it can't be behind the tapestry.

I estimated where the wall hanging was positioned, then started my search at around eye level. Alder was only a few inches taller than me. It took almost a minute, but finally my fingers felt loose dirt around a stone. I pulled it out and smiled at my ingenuity. Freyr and Stefan would now have a window into the great hall. I just hoped Alder wouldn't notice it.

I dropped down through the opening and into the creepiest place I'd ever been. Dark tunnels branched off in every direction. Even if I'd had the time to look around, wandering around medieval dungeons alone was not something I relished. Not wanting to waste time, and really not wanting to get freaked out, I took off my white T-shirt and used the pen to scrawl a message. Then I got back to my room and resumed my coma.

I had done what I could. The rest was up to Freyr. If I knew my mate, he and the others were already in Germany, willing to go to any lengths to get to me. I prayed that in finding me, we weren't going to lose someone else.

CHAPTER NINETEEN—FREYR

We were in the air three hours after the call from Germany. Traveling with me were Stefan and Sam, Greta and Kirner, and Quincy and Lowner. We also brought a clean-up team to deploy after we'd secured Carter. I wasn't going to let a single one of Alder's vampires get away. Not this time.

During the flight, Stefan and I discussed the best strategy for approaching Drubich. Lowner and Quincy were fighting in whispers, which didn't surprise me. Quincy was pissed when his mate refused to stay home.

Kirner hadn't bothered suggesting Greta stay behind. He and his new mate were silent, clutching each other's hands. Suddenly, he turned to face Greta, then got down on one knee while cramped between the airplane seats. She stared at him, dumbfounded, as he took her hands in his. "Sweet Greta, I love you and want to marry you. I had planned to do this in a much more romantic setting, but it has to be now, since we do not know what might happen in a few days. Will you marry me?"

Everyone in first class had turned to watch them, and for a minute I thought Greta was going to pass out before she could answer him. Then she smiled and said, "Yes. I don't care where or when you ask me. My answer has always been yes. I love you."

He kissed her hands. "I love you, too, and I have your ring, but you may not want to wear it if—"

"Gimme," she demanded.

Kirner shook his head and laughed. He reached up into his

156

carry-on and retrieved a small box. Greta opened it and squealed. "It's so beautiful. Oh, Kirner. Thank you."

I saw Kirner glance at Sam and mouth, "Thank you." I had no doubt the latter had selected the ring.

Stefan scowled at Sam. "You knew about this and didn't tell me? I'm crushed."

"My head would have been crushed if I said anything. I was intimidated into secrecy."

While I was thrilled for Greta, her happiness reminded me of how much I stood to lose if this mission failed. I looked out the window at the twinkling dots of color that lit the city of Munich. I tapped my foot nervously, and Stefan put a hand on my shoulder. "We'll get him back, Frey. Have faith."

"Thanks, old friend," I said. Then I whispered, "But if something happens and we don't get to him before . . . If we're too late, just promise me one thing."

"What's that?"

"Kill me, Stefan. If Carter's already gone, promise me you'll kill me."

He looked at Sam, as if considering what he'd want in the same circumstance. What would he do if he lost Sam forever? With a trembling chin, he looked at me and nodded.

After we got the clean-up team checked into the hotel, Stefan, Kirner, Quincy, and I met in my room to discuss strategy. Greta, Lowner, and Sam had gone out to find an Army surplus store to get extra supplies.

Stefan said, "I can only imagine what Greta's going to do to charm them into forking over knives and tactical gear, and God knows what else."

"She can pay for them," I said. "I gave her the black card."

"But . . . she asked for mine too," Stefan said in surprise.

"And mine," Quincy said with a scowl.

We all looked at Kirner, who cocked his head to one side.

"Do you have to ask?"

Quincy shook his head. "So she has plenty of money, but wouldn't you be suspicious if Greta, Sam, and Lowner walked into your store and asked to be fitted out for the Apocalypse?"

I snorted and burst into laughter. "It sounds like a joke! A blond, an Egyptian, and a butler walk into a bar . . ."

We all lost it, and the stress relief was wonderful. I made a mental note to tell the story to Carter when he was safely back in my arms. I wasn't going to say "*if* he was back." I absolutely refused to say "if."

Once we'd regained our composure, Stefan took a large piece of paper from his briefcase and unfolded it on the table. "This is a plan of the castle drawn from a satellite image, but it's pretty vague, so Freyr, can you give us as much intel as you can?"

I blew my bangs off my forehead. "I'll try." We spent the next hour and a half going over the schematics of the castle. I did the best I could, but there were gaps in my memory.

"I'm sorry," I said dejectedly.

"Don't beat yourself up, Frey," Stefan said. "For Christ's sake, you haven't been there in over five hundred years. I can't remember anything about it."

Greta, Sam, and Lowner returned with four bellhops, each laden with bags upon bags of clothing and gear. The humans trailed after Greta like wolves drooling after a sheep. After putting the bags down, they all turned to her and stared.

"Thanks boys," she said with a giggle. Then she grabbed Kirner's wallet from his back pocket and handed each of her adoring minions twenty euros. They all smiled and thanked her, but when they saw Kirner put a possessive hand on her shoulder, they fairly ran for the door.

Kirner held out his hand, and Greta placed his wallet in it. Then she batted her eyelashes at him. He crossed his arms and glared.

"You shouldn't tease him like that," Lowner said.

She waved away the comment. "Just show Freyr what you got for him, which—I might add—Lowner was able to purchase by seducing the salesman at the store."

"*Lowner* did?" Stefan asked.

"God, yes." Sam chuckled. "That poor man. He's probably still standing there, questioning his sexuality."

Quincy grabbed his mate around the waist. "His seductive powers will bring even the straightest man to his knees. Literally."

Lowner shoved him away. "This is important, you oaf." He looked at me, nervously wringing his hands.

"What is it?" I asked.

"W-when we were getting the knives and everything, I saw something that I thought—oh, I don't know what I was thinking. Never mind. It's stupid."

Greta held up a long narrow bag and said, "Lowner, show him or I will."

Lowner sighed. "I remembered your stories of what had happened at the castle all those years ago and I thought this would be a good way to end it. And I remember you used to be really good, but if you don't want it, I'll completely—"

"Lowner, let me see what it is." He handed me the bag. I unzipped it and gasped. It was a bow and a quiver of arrows. I removed the contents and laid them out on the table. Removing an arrow, I ran my thumb along the feathers and looked at Lowner.

"See," Lowner whined. "It's such a stupid idea."

The thought that Lowner had put into such a gift was astounding. It was a big risk on his part—and risks were not something he ever indulged in. I replaced the arrow in the quiver and pulled Lowner into an embrace.

"Thank you," I said. "This means a lot."

He was flustered and embarrassed and shocked that I'd hugged him, so he made an excuse to leave the room. Quincy followed him, and I could hear their murmured terms of affection. Kisses soon followed, as well as sounds of a more intimate nature.

We all stared at each other in an embarrassed silence until Sam cleared his throat and said, "I didn't know you were an archer."

"I wasn't really, but we all knew how to shoot. When we first moved to New York, I had a target. It's probably still somewhere around the house."

"All right," Stefan said. "Let's all sit down and decide how to do this."

We began brainstorming, but with little progress. Five minutes later, Lowner came out of their room looking completely rumpled. Quincy followed him, with a disgustingly smug grin on his face.

"Damn," Greta said with a laugh. "That was the quickest and quietest blow job in history."

Quincy winked at her, and Lowner huffed. "Can we just get on with it?"

"That's what he said," Quincy teased. He goosed his mate, who crossed the room and sat between Stefan and me.

"Seriously, guys," Stefan said. "Somehow we've got to get in there without attracting a lot of attention. It's not like we can climb over the walls."

A thought occurred to me then and I chuckled. "We can't go over the walls," I said, "but we can sure as hell go under them."

Kessler Wood looked eerily similar to when I'd left five centuries before. I expected it to be completely overgrown, or cleared for houses and development. Yet when I stopped at the edge of the trees, and saw the castle in the distance, it was exactly as it had been so many years before.

Stefan put his mouth right to my ear and whispered, "Carter's up there, Frey. You're so close. We can do this."

"Yeah. Let's find the door to the tunnels."

I knew the relative position of the original door, but there was no guarantee it would still be there. In fact, there was no guarantee the tunnel was there. It might have collapsed, or been filled in. We searched in a straight line from the edge of the wood until Lowner raised his fist. I knelt and dug away at the layers of dirt and leaves until I found an iron hinge.

Relief washed over me, and I cleared the door of debris. The rusted hinges disintegrated with very little pressure, but door still squeaked a little. We quickly piled through and closed it again, leaving just a few inches as an escape route. I checked the map as we went, and we got lost a few times, but finally I came upon a sight that nearly made me weep.

A rope ladder hanging from an opening in a wooden floor. It was the hidden entrance to the great hall. Better than that, though, was the white T-shirt I found tied to a rung. There was writing on it:

Door's open. Took out stone so you'll have a view. I'm fine, not locked up. Alder's due back this eve. Gave me ivas but it doesn't do much. I'm pretending to be weak. 15 vamps in here but I can help you. I know about what I can do and I can control it now. They don't know, tho. Dinner every night at 7. Maybe then? I'm not good at that part of planning. Can't wait to see you. Love you and be careful!

PS did you leave Goodnight Moon w/dog sitter to read to Titus?

I chuckled at his postscript, then held the shirt to my nose and inhaled. The wonderful, sweet, fruity scent of my mate filled my lungs, and such a weight lifted off my shoulders that I thought I would fly. All we had to do was wait for dinner to start. Then I'd go in and fight for my mate.

Chapter Twenty—Carter

Alder ran his fingers through my hair. "Sleep well, pet?"
I sat up slowly and yawned. "Without you in the room, I slept like a baby."

"Come on, you're late for dinner."

"You do realize," I said, while pulling on my shoes, "that this isn't the headquarters for the Third Reich? Ease up a little before you shit a brick."

"Mind your manners."

"No. I don't want to mind my fucking manners. In fact, I want to try and see how many fucking times I can say *fuck*, or any variant thereof, before you completely fucking lose your shit, so fuck you! Fuckety, fuck, fuck! Ow!"

The slap didn't really hurt that much, but I still went into moody, pissed-off, grounded-for-life emo-kid mode. "Whatever! You can't stop me from doing what I want. As soon as I'm eighteen, I'm outta this dump!"

He paused and smiled. "You're so witty. Well, I can't wait to wipe that smug look off your face when you see who's on the menu tonight."

"Who?" I mumbled. Holy shit, did he mean people? Suddenly, I didn't think I could keep going. I couldn't imagine what horror awaited me. Alder shoved me forward, and I walked numbly toward the great hall. My stomach turned when I saw three young girls being held by Caroline, Barney, and Klaus. The girls couldn't have been any older than sixteen, and one of them was whimpering for her mother.

"You sick fuck!" I screamed. "They're just kids! Let them

go, Alder. If you're so damned desperate to get back at me, you've already succeeded. If you want me to beg for my life, so be it. If you want my body, you can have it. Just let them go."

I was terrified, and wished that Freyr was there to help me. I couldn't do this myself.

Please find me, babe! I'm so scared.

Alder smirked. "Come here. Then I will release them."

As anxious as I was to save the girls, I was a fool to believe Alder. As soon as I stepped closer to him, he drove a dagger deep into my chest. I staggered backward and watched in horror as the girls were all bitten in the throat.

For the first time since becoming immortal, the smell of blood made me sick. These girls were dying and there was nothing I could do to help them.

I fell to my knees and doubled over in pain. The wound was excruciating, but an odd sensation was overriding the initial shock. The torn flesh was healing around the knife. I pulled the blade free and dropped it on the floor. Then I opened my shirt to check the wound.

It wasn't there. It had healed almost instantly.

That's when the pieces of the puzzle clicked. I was so powerful — nearly invincible. I could cook people's minds without even looking at them. I could practically fly. I really was a hybrid of some sort. That was it. Alder had said we'd been mated, and I'd even been given his blood while I was in the hospital, but I was truly mated to Freyr and had taken his blood many times. It seemed impossible, but I knew it must be true. My blood was bonding with *both* brothers' cells. I had developed all of their formidable strengths, and apparently powers which they didn't possess.

It was time to let my beast out. I got to my feet and took my shirt off. As I brushed my hands over my pecs. Alder's jaw dropped, and he said in shock, "But . . . I stabbed you!"

"Yes, you did." I hissed, taking a step toward him.

For the first time since I'd known him, Alder shied away from me. He was scared.

"What *are* you?" he breathed.

"I'm you," I said, with a seductive smile. "Like you said, I'm your mate. The problem is, I'm also Freyr's mate. Did you consider what might happen if my blood bonded with yours *and* your brother's?"

"B-both?" he stuttered.

My eyes blazed. "The whole is greater than the sum of its parts."

As I looked into his eyes, I focused my thoughts on the guards around the perimeter of the room. It didn't take very much effort. They all dropped to the floor, clutching their heads and screaming.

The noise distracted me for just a moment, and Alder took his chance. He took another dagger from the display cases behind him and went for my throat. I thought I was about to die, but the air was cut with a loud whoosh, and Alder staggered backward. The dagger dropped to the floor. He looked in disbelief at the arrow in the center of his chest.

The tapestry which hid the entrance to the tunnels was ripped down, and Freyr stepped into the great hall, bow in hand.

"Freyr!" I cried.

"It can't be you!" Alder panted in disbelief. His eyes grew wide as a second arrow flew. Bone crunched under the missile's impact. It struck him just above his collarbone, on the right side of his body. Another arrow struck him in the left ribcage. Another struck his stomach and the next pierced his right arm. The last planted itself deep inside Alder's heart. He gasped for air before slumping sideways.

Freyr crossed the room, smashed the glass of the display, and grabbed the priest's sword. He prepared to swing, but I wanted my revenge as well. I needed to have a hand in

Alder's death.

I said, "Stop, Freyr. I want to kill him."

Alder looked at me and coughed weakly. Blood trickled from his lips. "Why do you want to do it?"

I fixed fiery gaze on his. "Because I can."

I swung the blade. Alder's head fell to the floor and rolled into a dusty corner. His body slumped sideways, and I thought my nightmare was over . . . until I saw Lowner rush to help the girls.

"Lowner, wait!" I cried.

Before I could stop him, Caroline snatched one of the daggers from the floor and flung it. A bright red arc sprayed onto the wall, and I saw Lowner sink to the floor. As he bled out from his artery, he seemed confused at what was happening.

He looked at his mate. "Quincy?"

Quincy roared in fury and grief. He and Stefan ran to his mate. Freyr flew at Caroline and tore her head off, while Sam and I took care of Barney and Klaus. Greta tried to help the girls, but they were already dead.

Lowner was on his back, and Stefan had his fingers held tight against the wound. He screamed, "Freyr, it's not healing fast enough. He's lost too much!"

Quincy leaned over his mate, sobbing. "Don't you leave me, Low. Don't you fucking leave me! I love you so much. Please, stay with me!"

Lowner smiled at him and spoke with slurred words. "S'okay . . . darling . . . I'll wait for you . . ." His bright green eyes began to fade.

"No! No! *No!*" Quincy cried. He looked around frantically, and picked up the knife. Freyr attempted to take it, but Quincy evaded him and tried to draw the blade over his own jugular.

"Stop him!" Greta shrieked.

Kirner tackled Quincy, who roared and fought against his

captor. "Let me go, damn you! I want to die. Please let me die. Oh my God, Lowner."

"No one is dying," Freyr barked. He knelt down and licked Lowner's throat to close the wound. "Jesus, he's lost a lot of blood. Greta, give me a bag."

Greta opened a small duffle, and I was shocked to see it filled with IV bags of synthetic blood. It was a relatively new technology, and we all drank it once in a while. The taste was lousy compared to my mate's blood, but it was better than nothing. As far as I knew, it hadn't been given to anyone in large quantities.

Greta held a bag up above Lowner and handed the tube to Freyr. She asked, "You know what you're doing?"

"No. Quince, you gotta talk me through this." He looked at the stricken doctor and whistled to get his attention. "Tell me what to do, and use simple words, okay?"

Quincy nodded numbly. "I'll do it." With a shaky breath, he grabbed the bag from Freyr and had the IV hooked up in seconds. Then he grabbed the bag of blood from Freyr.

"Is it gonna work?" I asked frantically.

"We'll make it work," Quincy said. He squeezed the bag, forcing the life-saving synthetic blood into his mate's system. There was no change for about a minute, but then Lowner's eyes shot open, swirling red. When he tried to grab the IV, Sam sat on one of his arms, and I sat on the other.

Quincy sobbed out a laugh, "Just hold still, Low. You're going to be fine." Quincy handed the bag to Freyr, then knelt by his mate's prone form. Lowner tried to talk, but Quincy stopped him, "Ssh, don't talk. Just heal."

When the danger had passed, we took the heads off all of Alder's crew and carried the bodies outside to burn. Stefan had the gruesome task of photographing the young girls so we could find out who they were. He'd use his connections within the intelligence community to find their names.

I stood over the girls' bodies and said a short prayer. Freyr came up behind me. He wrapped his arm around me, but I jerked away.

"It's all my fault," I sobbed. "These girls died because of me. Lowner almost died because of me."

"No," Freyr replied sternly. He took me by the shoulders and forced me to look at him. "Those girls died because of Alder. You did nothing wrong, you hear me?"

"I was so scared," I mumbled. "He kept calling me his mate, and I was so afraid I'd forget you."

He stroked my hair. "No matter what happened, or what you did, I will always love you. You are my eternal mate, and nothing can change that."

I looked down in shame and confessed, "On the plane here, I killed two men."

His hand stopped stroking my back, and he clutched me tighter. "Oh, my love. I'm so sorry. But you're still a good person, Carter. Never forget that."

My strength finally left my body, and I crumpled into his arms. He carried me to a large SUV and tucked me into the passenger's seat. After a gentle kiss, he went to help do a final sweep of the building. Once the castle had been cleared, we drove toward Munich. I didn't look back.

We left Germany five days later. Lowner had recovered rapidly, though he would have done so much more quickly if he wasn't constantly bickering with Quincy. When we got home to New York, the two of them went to their room and didn't emerge for several days, except for the occasional drink or snack. The dogs made messes in the kitchen, dining room, drawing room, and library, but even then Lowner didn't rush in with carpet cleaner and surgical mask.

We went through Alder's papers and discovered that his "higher-learning center" was in fact going to be a vampire breeding farm. Anyone who wanted to become a vampire could come there and fulfill their twisted dreams. If he'd completed his plans, he could have built a vampire army. There was already a list of five hundred people due to start their transition the following spring. The list of the vampire-wannabes was handed over to Interpol, and many people were taken into custody. It was gratifying to know not only did we get justice for all that Alder had done to us and our families, but we also prevented the deaths of thousands of people who would have fallen under his spell.

As Alder's only relative, Freyr inherited the entire estate, which was larger than any of us had ever imagined. We gave the macabre collection of family relics to the Berlin Museum, and provided funds for new galleries to house their Medieval Art collection. We also funded several archaeological digs around southern Germany.

Several months later, after all of the legal matters were taken care of, Freyr and I made the final trip to his ancient home. There was one more thing he wanted to do. We stood together among the larch trees and watched while Drubich Castle was demolished.

EPILOGUE

Six Years Later

Freyr came into the kitchen one morning and said, "Carter, I have something to ask you."

I didn't look up from the newspaper on the table in front of me. "Hm?"

He sighed. "Could you look at me, please?"

"Hang on." I filled in the last answer on my crossword and glanced at him. "What's up?"

"Well, what I have to say is—"

"'Scuse me," Greta chirped as she scooted between my mate and me to take the only empty seat at the table.

Freyr began again. "Okay. It's—"

He was interrupted again when Lowner stepped in front of him, and set a plate in front of me. "Here's your muffin. Hot from the oven."

"Oh, for fuck's sake." Freyr shoved Lowner out of the way and scowled.

I picked up my fork and tore into the pastry. It was mouth-watering. "Lowner, you are a magician. These blueberries just burst with—"

"Carter!"

I swallowed a bite of blueberry muffin and put my fork down. "Sorry, honey."

Freyr raised an eyebrow. "Do I have your attention now?"

"Yes."

"Good. Now, everyone else, shut up and don't move."

Then he exhaled sharply, and dropped to one knee. My mouth fell open.

"Oh my God," I mumbled.

Freyr smiled. "Babe, I love you more than anything. We've worked so hard for what we have together, and I can't think of a better way to celebrate that than to get married. Will you be my husband?"

I launched myself at my mate and he fell back onto the floor. Quincy laughed. "I guess that's a *yes.*"

"Hell yeah, that's a *yes,*" I said, and took Freyr's mouth with my own. I kissed him and licked his throat until a loud cough reminded me we had an audience.

"To be continued later," Freyr promised. We stood and straightened our clothes. Freyr took my chair and pulled me down onto his lap. Everyone congratulated us, and Lowner practically skipped out into the garden to retrieve ingredients for a grand, celebratory meal.

A few minutes later, however, the garden door slammed open. Lowner stormed into the kitchen, dragging a muddy, stinking bundle behind him.

"Greta!" he boomed. "I've had it up to here with him! Last week it was an entire collection of Irish crystal, the week before that it was the chandelier in the dining room. This week he's wreaked havoc in the garden! He has pulverized my polyanthus!"

Everyone snorted and choked, trying not to laugh, but it was impossible. We all burst out laughing at Lowner's hysterical rant. He narrowed his eyes and thrust the guilty party at Greta. She put her hands up to keep the mud off her dress.

"What do you have to say for yourself?" she asked.

One purple eye was visible under the curtain of mud-caked hair. He looked at her and said, "Hi, Mom."

She sighed. "Did you really trample the flowers?"

"Um, yes, but not really."

Just then Kirner came through the door. When he saw the state of his son, he turned on his heel and went right back out.

"Get in here!" Greta snapped.

Her husband sheepishly returned to the kitchen and looked severely at his dripping son. "What have you done?"

The five-year-old terror cleared his throat and began his recitation. "I was playing spy, and the dogs were my other spies, but Ramesses ran away through the garden. I had to catch him."

"Why did he run away?" Sam asked warily.

"'Cause they gotta blend with the trees so the bad guys don't see us. So I painted 'em."

Greta crossed her arms on the table and put her head on them. Without looking up, she asked, "What did you paint them with?"

"Mud."

Sam's fists clenched, but only for a second. Like a defeated warrior, he said, "Come on, Kirner. We're on damage control."

Greta's eyes flashed at her son. "Look at your clothes. You're never going to come clean, you little imp."

His lip stuck out a foot, and he began to wail. Being the softie that I was, I went to him and hugged him, immediately feeling the grime soak through my shirt. I pushed back his gold-blond hair and those violet eyes melted into mine.

"I'm sorry, Uncle Carter," he said shakily. "Sorry, Uncle Freyr."

My mate could never resist the little boy's pout, and neither could I. I took his filthy hand in mine and chuckled. "Come on, Jake. Time for a bath."

ABOUT THE AUTHOR

Kazy Reed grew up on a small island off the Maine Coast. At the age of sixteen, she announced to her parents that she was going to move to Denmark as an exchange student. That trip changed her life, and sparked her love of travel, languages, and history.

After graduating from college in Massachusetts with a degree in Art History, she moved back to Maine, where she began to write short stories. When she was introduced to gay erotic fiction, the seed was planted and she never looked back.

Kazy still lives in Southern Maine, with her very understanding husband and two ridiculously precocious children.